Bram Stoker's
Irving

by
Terry Cunningham

Bram Stoker's Irving

by
Terry Cunningham

First published 2002
First reprint 2003
Enlarged and revised 2nd edition published 2004

by
Stagedoor Publishing
London, WC1N 3XX, UK

www.zoism.co.uk

Printed and typeset in the EEC

Front cover portrait by Michael Shaw

Mike has achieved cult status as an artist in recent years
with his very distinctive style that he describes as a mix
of contemporary graphic and 'Rock and Roll'.
His portraits of Elvis, Dean, Monroe, Clift, Brando
(and now Irving) and many others are known the world over.
He lives and works in London.

THIS BOOK IS DEDICATED
TO THOSE WHO KNOW
THE HANDS ON THE CLOCK
DO NOT TELL THE REAL TIME

Other works by the same author:

Travels on the 'Hound'

South Across the River

The Great '78s

The President Demands Maximum Attack

Geronimo's Cadillac

Pacific Graveyard

James Dean. The Way It Was

14 – 18 The Final Word

A sketch made by the author of Henry outside the Lyceum,
January 1879

Note from Robert Appleby,

Director, Stagedoor Publishing, London

As a publisher there is something I must explain about this book that will, I am sure, make it an even more enjoyable and interesting read.

When I first published it abroad, I knew almost nothing about the theatrical world of Henry Irving or his era. Since then, it's been pointed out to me by many eminent people, among them Professor Koolhaas-Remer who lives in Amsterdam and is a renowned theatrical historian, that it is historically correct in every detail.

The following is an extract from one of his letters: "I have studied the times and events that this book covers for over 40 years yet there are things mentioned that I knew nothing about, so I carried out more detailed research and, to my amazement, they have proved to be correct. Every statement made by a character that the reader would regard as just a casual remark about what someone is wearing or what he or she said, a date, time or place is incredibly accurate. In fact, I now realise that in this book there are no casual remarks.

I enclose, for your interest, a separate list of one hundred examples of minute details that I know, after a lifetime studying the subject, are totally accurate.

I know nothing about the author or his girlfriend, but with respect they do not sound the sort of people who would spend their lives studying Victorian theatre! The book tells an exciting story, but on another level. Knowing the subject matter as I do I found it mystifying and unnerving."

These are a few random examples from the professor's list… How on earth did he know the name of the shop in Bond Street before 'Asprey'. Or the last words of Gordon Craig and William Terriss. It was the 1,897th performance of Novello's show. Ellen Terry's horse was called Tommy and the mayor she waved to was a Mr Stileman in 1901. The details of the gold casket and book presented to Irving are perfect, as are the descriptions of the interiors of Irving's apartment, Stokers house and the Lyceum. Irving's tailor was indeed Henry Poole. Prince, the man who murdered Terriss, was dressed exactly like that and he did have a pronounced squint!

Foreword
by Sir John Gielgud

In early 2000, a few months before his death, I sent a draft of this book to Sir John at his home near Aylesbury. I had worked with him on two occasions in the 1970s and knew he was the great nephew of Ellen Terry; therefore, the subject would interest him. I always found him approachable and helpful and his reply proves it. I have edited out parts of the letter that do not relate to the book. He states that an actor friend, who is a weekend guest, has read it to him twice; he found it so enjoyable and being rather frail at 95 the same friend will type his letter of reply. He adds it will then be "far more readable than my awful handwriting."

Thank you, dear Robert, for sending this fascinating story. Like you, I miss those years. The London we so adored I regret no longer exists and is only inhabited by the ghosts of those we loved. Every actor of my generation admired Irving tremendously and I think to a great extent lived in his shadow, so to read a work like this brings him back in an original and indeed strange and violent way. I do so like the way the author moves from awful modern 'new speak' to the language used by those of Irving's day. Many of the events mentioned were told to me by Ellen Terry herself and, as far as I know, were never made public. Did they go back in time? I leave that for your readers to decide. Now I have reached this great age, I accept things I cannot prove or disprove. I keep asking M...... to re-read parts of it, then I say, my word yes! I recall Ellaline Terriss, daughter of William, telling me that back in the 1920s. The facts revealed by the author are really quite extraordinary. This will renew the legend of Irving and the Lyceum and all the wonderful artists of that time. If I had read this forty years ago, I would have purchased the film rights, cast myself in the role of Irving and, of course, Vivien would play Ellen Terry, and what a wonderful Bram Stoker Larry would have been and by now, of course, it would be regarded as a film classic!

My kindest regards to you, Robert

John

Sir John Gielgud

Bram Stoker's Irving

In July 1951 Sir Laurence Olivier was asked to open the new gardens around Sir Henry Irving's statue. In his speech he said:

"He died two years before I was born and yet I feel as close to him as if I had been a member of his company. I feel his presence every time I step on the stage."

"I believe in immortality and my belief is strengthened with advancing years. Without faith in things spiritual this life would, indeed, be a weary waste."

Sir Henry Irving

Chapter One

Explain the following events? I cannot. I can only relate them as they happened and hope you find my story of interest. In my mind I am still confused as to when it all took place; it is as clear as yesterday yet the calendar and history tell me it was over a century ago. Bear with me as I try to give you an idea of where I am coming from – and just for the record I do not do drugs nor drink to any excess and, until now, I had never seen a ghost or had any interest in the paranormal. Maybe I am still too close to it all to try and put it down on paper, but I must because I want to recall this incredible and, to me, terrifying story while it is still fresh in my mind; with clarity and not with long distance hindsight. One thing I now know for sure is that we are surrounded by happenings and forces that are totally beyond our comprehension in this short life of ours.

Who am I? Not much to tell really; I'm middle aged, divorced and I live in a small flat that doubles as my office in Soho – that area of central London famous for clubs, crime, gangsters, prostitution, and all-round low-down nightlife in general (none of which, I regret to say, I have had much dealings with in all my years of being here). For a living I run a small one-man-band theatrical agency. If you want a singer, dancer, stuntman, actor or even lion tamer, then I will have one on my books for you. That's how I met Lee. She was singing karaoke in south London pubs and doing some pole dancing; now I get her gigs in West End clubs. I think she is more sexy than talented, but that is between us. I also have a passion for old American cars that I can't afford and I have Lee, who I can afford even less, mainly because she is less than half my age. She lives, or maybe I should say, lived in Peckham down in Southeast London. Her full name is Letitia Rudge. She came down from Birmingham as a teenager. We have our own places because we like our space, and she looks after my car at her place because there is no way you can park here in Beak Street (just a 100yds from Regent Street where I am writing this). Let me also add that I am not a fan of the theatre and know little about it – I much prefer going to a movie or, better still, watching a film at home.

I will now relate what happened as simply as I can, but it will not be easy. Maybe you or someone out there who reads this may have an explanation for it all; I certainly do not and my biggest fear is I never will. If I go over it any more in my mind I will lose what is left of my sanity. If you think you know the answer then be kind enough to let me know and I will be forever grateful. My long descent into the incredible came with an e-mail from Lee – a publisher pal of hers was starting a new book that he hoped was going to sell in it's millions worldwide. The working title was *The Greatest Star of All*. Apparently, it was to be about the life and career of the number one showbiz star of all time. The major problem was they had no idea who he or she was! Her pal wanted me, being on the fringe of showbiz, to advise him. She said that she would pick me up in my car at 9.00 pm. Lee signed off the e-mail with 'SOTLBALL' (it was our in-joke meaning 'She Of The Large Bust And Long Legs'). OK, so we all have our problems – mine is being silly about young women.

My car looked fantastic as Lee swung it into Golden Square. Back in 1955 when it was made Chrysler, the makers, called it the 'Beautiful Brute' and around fifty years later the C-300 with it's V.8 5ltr engine and two-tone blue bodywork stands out like a giant surrounded by the pygmies of today's small car world.

"Hop in, Tel, we're late," said Lee in that low husky voice of hers that reminded me of Lisabeth Scott, the movie star of the 1950's. I have never told her this because it would really date me and I had already knocked ten years off my age.

"Where's the meeting?" I asked.

"Over a strip club in Dean Street," she laughed.

"Christ, we could walk it."

Still laughing she yelled, "Shut your noise, you know I love driving this monster."

I got in and so began the strangest journey I or anyone

could ever undertake.

She handled the big left-hander like a mini and bullied her way through the late night traffic. When we got to the meeting it turned out I knew her publisher pal: it was Bob Appleby, he runs an outfit called 'Stagedoor'. I had written a couple of books for him a few years ago. Also, there was an old Irish guy I knew who worked as a photographer for Bob, called Danny Regan but known to one and all as Pad, who put a double whisky in my hand before I had even sat down. The room was packed. Most of those present struck me as pompous shits, so I ignored them.

"OK," said Bob, "you all know why we're here. I need to know the greatest star ever and I need to know fast. He or she must be an international star and remained so all their lives, never taking second billing. They can come from any era or time, but above all the public must love them. OK, let's go."

"Mickey Mouse," said Pad.

"Don't fuck about," yelled Lee. "This is big money."

"I'll have you know, my girl," retorted Pad, "he's been a star for eighty years, outlived all the rest and is still packing them in."

"He's a cartoon," said Bob. "I want real."

The names came thick and fast, but Bob cut them all down with rapid fire. Sinatra? Superb artist and what a voice, but was he loved with all that mafia stuff? Bing Crosby? Superb, from the 30s to the 50s, but the last twenty years he was semi-retired. I thought I had better say something, so I threw in Rudolf Valentino. He was magic on screen. The first world star and adored by moviegoers. Yes, but he died at 31. Same with James Dean – a real icon, but dead at 24 – so would they have lasted? We'll never know.

"So, hardly stars into their old age," said a little ponce in the corner who I suspected would like to nominate Danny La Rue. Someone said Al Jolson?

"Yes, that's getting close. The King of Broadway for 30 years. I'll put him down as a possible," said Bob.

Little ponce started to sulk.

"Elvis – the one and only," said an interesting looking guy standing by the window who I recognised as Mike Shaw, the artist famous for his portraits of classic movie stars.

"That's as close as we'll get, Mike," said Bob. "But there's already ten million books on him, what else is there to say?"

"The Beatles? The crafty scousers."

"No, there were four of them and they were never loved. There's nothing more dated than a 60s person," laughed Lee.

That alarmed me because I regarded myself as a 50s person!

"Come on, give me some names," said Bob with a hint of

panic in his voice.

"Cliff Richard!" I shot back.

"He fits the bill, but he's not international. He never cracked the American market."

"Rolling Stones?" Asked a lady almost timidly, who was sitting next to Pad.

"Boring old farts," yelled Lee.

Famous names were flying all over the room from stage, screen, radio, and even old time music hall.

"Laurence Olivier. I'll never forget his 1948 film version of Hamlet," said an elderly woman with sad eyes.

"Yes, but he had a great partner in Vivian Leigh," said Bob.

"Didn't Bogart have Bacall?" asked a voice.

"So what, Irving had Terry," mumbled Pad. Everyone looked blank.

"Who's that again?" asked Bob.

"Henry Irving, the greatest of all time," slurred Pad, whose head was now resting on the table.

"Pay no attention," said little ponce, "he's pissed out of his head."

"And you're a fucking arsehole," said Pad, putting on what I thought was an extra strong Irish accent.

"That's enough of that," yelled Bob, placing the whisky bottle back in his drawer.

To lower the tension I threw in the name Liz Taylor, always a worldwide star and lived like one too.

"Thanks, Tel, I'll put her down, she's way up on the list. Yes, nice one, born in London too."

However, I sensed that we had still not found that elusive person that covered all Bob's publishing needs or maybe dreams.

It was well gone midnight, so I was pleased when Pad gave me the excuse I wanted by asking if I would drop him off at his flat near Covent Garden. Lee, who had been tapping into her laptop all evening now logged off. I gathered up my notes. We each took one of Pad's arms as we said our goodnights. Bob called after me, "Call me soon. I need help on this one."

With Pad sprawled on the wide backseat of the Chrysler and Lee behind the wheel, we took off into the teeming rain with streaks of vivid white lightning forking through the black sky.

"Shit, this is like driving in a monsoon. Where's your place Pad, or are you still pissed?" she asked.

"No, I'm not, me girl. It's off Wellington Street, I'll direct you, but first I want you to cut down this side street on the left."

Lee gave me that half smile that meant 'now what'. We came out near Leicester Square, next to a large statue of an elegant looking man who looked like he had been there a long time.

"Do you know where we are, Tel, me boy?"

"Yes, Paddy, I do. We're in Irving Street and just for the record you're becoming irritating."

"Don't be rude to Pad or I'll dump you for him," said Lee.

"You could do worse," laughed Pad. Pointing at the statue he said, "That's the man Bob wants for his book – the greatest name in the history of acting. He topped the bill at the Lyceum Theatre for forty years and took his entire company all over the world. Ellen Terry, the greatest actress of her time, was his leading lady. All the great names of the time acted with him or were in his company. He was the first actor to be knighted and he's buried in Westminster Abbey. His manager, friend and right-hand man for all those years was Bram Stoker, the author of Dracula. For years he, and the talented crowd he had around him, made London the world's centre for show business in all its forms."

Lee lowered the window and despite the driving rain read aloud the words on the base of the statue.

"HENRY IRVING.
ACTOR. BORN 1838. DIED 1905.
LITT.D.DUBLIN.D.LITT.CAMBRIDGE.LL.D.GLASGOW.
ERECTED BY ENGLISH ACTORS AND ACTRESSES
AND BY OTHERS CONNECTED WITH THE THEATRE
IN THIS COUNTRY."

"What Bob would call one hell of a star, how come you know so much about him?" I asked.

"I took his photo by mistake many years ago and until today I was still mystified."

As I knew she would, Lee said, "Tell us more because even you weren't around a hundred years ago."

"No. It was July 1939, the Lyceum was being closed down because the Second World War was about to start and John Gielgud and Fay Compton were appearing there in Hamlet. Gielgud was the great nephew of Ellen Terry and he came on stage at the end and made a speech saying: 'God Bless the Lyceum, Henry Irving and Ellen Terry.' Very moving it was; we all stood and cheered him, little did we know we were facing six long years of war. Anyway, I took some photos outside the theatre and when I'd developed them, there was Irving, who had been dead some thirty-four years at the time, alighting from a horse-drawn cab with some other people. My wife was alive then and it frightened the hell out of her. She begged me to keep quiet about it."

"Do you still have the photo, Pad?"

"I do, Lee, and I want you to have it. You'll find it interesting because you will recognise the people with Irving. After all these years I've only just realised who they are – it's because they're dressed in the style of those days – that's what threw me."

"Pad, what are you going on about? How the shit would I know anyone in that photo?"

"You'll believe me when you see it. Indeed you will, my girl."

Just then, the sound of yelling and shouting came from Charing Cross Road. Heading in our direction were a crowd of yobs, one with a pit bull dog on a rope lead, all wearing reverse baseball caps.

"Trouble," said Pad.

"Big trouble," I agreed.

"Hold on lady, 'old on," said the one with a thin spiteful face. "Gonna give us a ride in the flash motor?"

"No chance, scumbag," yelled Lee.

Scumbag and Co did not like that one bit. Thin face jumped onto the heavy front bumper. Lee slipped the gearshift into reverse, and slammed her dainty high-heeled shoe down hard. The old V8 went back like a freight train then pulling like hell on the hand brake, with smoke coming from the huge white-wall tyres, we did a screaming hand brake turn like you only see in the movies. Scumbag was flung off like a rag doll and we hope badly injured. As a couple of cider bottles sailed over our roof and smashed against the wall of the National Portrait Gallery we screamed off towards the Strand with the acceleration forcing me back in my seat.

"For Christ's sake slow down, Lee, you can't drive a motor

this size like a Porsche!"

She answered me in that sweet way of hers. "Tell me about it, wanker, just cos you drive it like a hearse."

Looking over her shoulder, she gave Pad a sexy wink, and then in a singsong voice said, "It's 20 foot long, 7 foot wide, weighs over 2 tons and can top 110 mph."

"Jesus, I haven't enjoyed myself so much in years," laughed Pad as we pulled in by the drab council block where he lived. "Trouble is though, if you've killed that young thug the fuzz will have no problem tracing this eye catching yank monster."

"Frankly, my dear Pad, I don't give a damn," she laughed with that hint of devilment I loved.

"I'll get that photo, hold on a second, my friends," said Pad still laughing.

Lee told me to go with him in case of muggers. At his door he handed me an envelope, then looking sad he shook my hand saying, "Don't let today's awful world get you down, my boy."

I dived back into the car trying to avoid the driving rain. Looking back at Pad as he stood framed in the lighted doorway with his arm raised, dramatically he called out. "Now cracks a noble heart, goodnight, sweet prince and may flights of angels sing thee to thy rest!"

With the sound of thunder crashing across the sky we drove

away fast. "I just love that old guy," said Lee. "What was that he called out?"

"It's a quotation from Hamlet – that's a play by Shakespeare in case you've never heard of it – and my place is in the other direction." I reminded her as I put Paddy's envelope in the glove compartment.

"I was going to cut over Waterloo Bridge and take you down to my place, thought you might fancy a night of wild, way-out sex. Yesterday, I got a new basque and high heels, but if you'd rather not I'll turn right at the next lights."

"No, head for the bridge – you talked me into it."

With Lee I always had that feeling of I really ought not to be doing this, but then I suppose that only added to the thrill that I got from being with her. One day, of course, she'd find a much younger man and I would miss her forever, but until then I would try and keep up with her. Already there had been a couple of times when I had not been able to rise to the occasion and she had laughed it off, but for how long?

"Why have we stopped?" I had to shout because the sound of hailstones hitting the roof was deafening.

"It's no good, I just can't see. You only have single speed wipers on this old bus and they're not clearing the screen fast enough. We'll sit here 'til it clears a bit."

With that, she leaned over and gave me a long slow French

kiss. "That's just a trailer for the big movie coming later and cum you will," she whispered in that husky voice. Then pulling away said, "Lets have some music. Oh, shit! The storm's knocked out the radio, or wireless as you call it." Giving me that half smile.

"Are we near the bridge?" I asked.

"Yeah, straight in front of us."

"Look out your window to the right and you'll see the Lyceum that Pad was going on about. God, it must have been an elegant theatre in its time. What a beautiful old place, those six tall columns, the huge doorway, if only it could talk, Lee."

"You can bet some bastard is planning to knock it down and build an office block."

"While we're waiting look up this Irving on your laptop, see if there's any info about him."

"I doubt it," she laughed.

Opening the lid of the small case, her fingers flew over the keyboard, and then her face took on an amazed look as she slowly began to read the screen.

"Wow! Paddy was right, it's all here: he ran the Lyceum for over forty years; greatest actor of all time; had his own company of players; the great Ellen Terry was his leading lady; first actor ever to be knighted; took his whole company of actors, even the scenery, to America and toured coast-to-coast eight times. His first words on stage were: 'Here's to our enterprise', that was in 1856 when he appeared in Richelieu. He was only 18 years old. His last words on stage were: 'Into thy hands O'Lord, into thy hands', that's when he was playing 'Becket' in October 1905 when he was aged 67, and an hour after saying those words he was dead. One hell of a superstar! Could be the man Bob's looking for…there's more," said Lee in a wistful voice almost drowned out by the heavy rain still crashing on the Chryslers roof, "it's a sort of poem… 'Shakespeare whispered the secrets of great acting to Burbage, his favourite actor, he handed them on to Garrick, who gave them to Kean, who in turn told Irving, then on to Olivier and Gielgud, but the greatest of them all was Irving'. The last line is a knockout, get this, 'Henry Irving was the most beloved actor of all time.'"

She turned off the laptop, slumped back in her seat still staring at the blank screen in disbelief. "We must be a pair of know nothing prats! How come we never heard of him?" Before I could reply, she yelled again, "For Christ's sake, look at the dials!"

Staring at the old dashboard I saw the needles on the gas, oil and battery were all spinning wildly and the MPH told us that we were doing 90, yet we were parked with the engine off! Even the unique clock placed in the centre of the steering wheel was revolving backwards! At that moment, the sky blazed into light over the river; a rainbow of forked lightning floodlit the buildings and Waterloo Bridge; the windscreen became a wall of cascading rainwater as the thunder crashed and the howling wind rocked the old Chrysler on its huge tyres. Then I realised that inside the car we were in a soft blue light.

"I'm scared," said Lee clinging tightly round my neck (even at a time like that I remember the softness of her long hair brushing my face).

Within a minute or so all went quiet and for some strange reason I felt calm, a sort of peacefulness came over me. As Lee sat up straight she looked more beautiful than I have ever seen her. No longer sexy or streetwise – more elegant; she was the same yet a little older, almost serene, then quickly reverting to type.

"Shit, for the second time tonight we've got aggro. Here comes a mugger, London really is the pits."

Looking through the rain soaked side window I saw a very tall, strong looking man, well dressed, but in a strange old-fashioned style. He smiled, and then tapped lightly on the glass with a well-manicured hand bearing a large silver ring.

"We're out'er here, right now. Let's go," said Lee as she

turned the key. "For Christ's sake, the battery's dead. Must be this freak storm."

As my car is a left-hander I was on the kerbside nearest the guy, and with the power gone I could not drop the window, so slowly began to open the door. Lee grabbed my arm saying, "Tell the arsehole to fuck off now or he gets this."

She had taken from her bag a small nasty looking mace gas spray. "When he gets a face full of this, he'll be blind for a month." Seeing my look of horror she added, "Well, it comes in handy when I travel by tube at night, my last lover got it for me."

Makes my gifts of chocolates and undies seem very dated. To out-do any rivals remind me to make my next gift a stun gun!

I pushed the door wide open. The tall guy stepped forward smiling and extending his hand saying, "Good evening sir, madam, please join me for a tour of our lovely Lyceum Theatre."

He was loaded with charm, Irish charm by the sound of his accent.

"I'm from Dublin, but I live here in London now and will be happy to spend the rest of my days in the world's most elegant city."

He had answered my thoughts. How the hell did he do that?

Maybe he's a mind reading mugger.

"Allow me to introduce myself. I am Abraham Stoker, manager of the Lyceum Theatre and it's company of players. Also, I'm proud to say, a close friend of Mr Henry Irving."

Now out of the car, I realised the storm had passed and it had strangely changed to a clear dry night. Being a person who likes or dislikes people at first sight, I decided this guy was OK and was about to say who we were when, once again, he read my thoughts.

"I know all about both of you. Paddy has explained your quest to know who was the greatest talent of all, who lasted longer and was most loved by the public. The answer, my friends, is Henry Irving and if you'll permit me, I will now prove it to you."

"Just a minute, Abraham, how come you know Pad?" I asked.

"He joined us earlier this evening, he was old, tired and unhappy in the ugly London of your times. He's with his wife now, and is enjoying tranquillity. Oh, and do please call me Bram."

By now, Lee was out of the car and moving towards Bram with that aggressive walk of hers. For an awful moment I thought she was going to spray him with the mace. "Are you over the top polite or what, or maybe just taking the piss?"

Bram looked sad, as if he were sorry for us. "We come from very different times," he replied, "so my style of speech will seem odd to you, as yours does to me here in this time."

"OK," laughed Lee. "I'll buy it, what is your time and where exactly is here?"

"We are outside the Lyceum on the first night of Henry Irving playing Hamlet, it is Monday, 30th December and the year is 1878."

"Well, you did say exactly, Lee." I reminded her.

Bram continued. "All of London wants to see the greatest event in theatre history."

"Oh yeah! Tell me another thing. I'm a fan of gothic horror, are you the Bram Stoker who wrote Dracula?"

"I am indeed, madam, and I'm delighted that you have read my book."

"I haven't, but I saw the movie, and if I'm right, you wrote that in 1897. According to you that's nineteen years from now?"

"Yes, that's all correct. Please let me explain."

"Don't bother dickhead, I'd never take it in." Then turning to me she said. "That tear's it, this is a one hundred per cent nutter. How is it when I come out with you I end up in some insane situation? You stay with the car, I'll call a cab on my mobile."

"Wait, Lee," I said, grabbing her arm, more for my own reassurance than to stop her. "Take a look over there at the theatre."

We were both dazed at the sight before us. Wellington Street was now packed with several thousand noisy people. Three braziers over the portico of the Lyceum threw a warm glowing light over the surging crowds, long lines of horse-drawn carriages with noble crests on their door panels waited as well-dressed men and women were helped down by footmen as good humoured cockneys cheered.

"Every walk of London life is here," said Bram, "but most will not be lucky enough to get a seat tonight. The pit and the gods sold out hours ago." Then smiling he added. "What you would call, sir, the front stalls and the upper circle."

Lee looked on in total disbelief. "Where the hell did this lot come from? It's like a scene from a movie; that's it isn't it, Tel, they're making a movie? These are all extras and weirdo Bram here in fancy dress is an actor, right?"

"If that's the case, Lee, where's the camera crew, the lights. No this is more real than the dark miserable street we drove into minutes ago."

Bram moved closer holding out his arms as if to embrace us saying, "Don't be alarmed, my dear friends, it is no dream, no trick of the light, you are here just as I am."

"Before I go all out ape shit," shouted Lee to make herself heard above the noise of the crowd and the clatter of horses. "How come no one in this crowd from, as you say, 1878 takes a second glance at me in my mini skirt, holding a laptop, Tel's leather jacket or our car? Answer me that smart arse Bram."

Quietly and politely he began to do just that. "Because they see you in a long dress and picturesque hat with feathers; your magic box to them is a parasol; your motorised machine appears as a gleaming black landau drawn by four fine horses with a top hatted coachman at the reins." Then turning to me he added, "You, sir, are dressed the same as I, in a stylish frock coat made for you by Henry Poole, the finest tailors in Savile Row. Henry Irving and I have all our clothes made there. Come let me show you some highlights and events from the life and times of the greatest of all actors and his fellow thespians."

"Why are you so keen to show us all this, Bram?" I asked.

"Because you have almost no record of us, as was proved at that meeting you had earlier this evening. I want some memory of our time to travel into the twenty first century when you return to your time. And when you do, only a few hours will have passed, yet with me you will have spanned sixty years."

"Stupid question," said Lee, "but what the hell are you? A dead spirit who wants us to go back into the past or what?"

"I am what you would call a ghost, madam, but you must

understand that ghosts have memories and I am, as you will be for the next few hours, outside of time. You see there is no dead, no past or future. Time does not pass, it only moves around us. Life, death, past, future are at our side right here in the present. Nothing ever dies, it only changes."

"I'll need time to work all that out – call me back in ten years," said Lee.

Bram smiled, I think he was starting to like her. "Later tonight, madam, when on stage, Mr Irving will speak the following words by William Shakespeare. 'Who knows if to die be but to live, and that called life by us mortals is really death.'" He held out both his hands almost willing us to go with him. "Trust me, trust me," he said softly.

I hesitated, but Lee, changeable as ever, grabbed my arm excitedly saying, "Come on, let's go for it, we're both riders on the storm. Anyway, you know I love doing crazy things and this could be our ultimate trip. You hear what Bram's saying, this Irving guy weren't no one hit wonder, let's take a look at this superstar."

She knew I could refuse her nothing, so with Bram leading we beat a path through the surging mass of cheerful people who had come to the most famous theatre in Europe, or indeed, the world, to see the greatest actors of this or any age.

"You're witnessing the golden age of the Lyceum," Bram

called to us over his shoulder, "and it will last another thirty or more years."

As we got close, I noticed the six lofty columns supporting the roof were fluted. Bram, of course, read my thoughts saying. "They are in the Corinthian order, the two at each end are on the same base."

We passed into the magnificent hall all glitz, gold and gilt below a beautiful arched roof, then on into the vestibule with gold and white curtains from floor to ceiling. The walls were panelled with light rosewood and all the lighting was by gas, giving a warm glowing effect. Above us hung a huge glass chandelier suspended by ten massive glass cords, the light reflected through hundreds of crystal glass icicles. The overall sight of the auditorium was spellbinding. Each side of the forty-foot wide stage ran rows of boxes with red velvet curtains. The stalls consisted of row upon row of gold backed seats, now packed with a highly excited and noisy audience.

"Come, my friends," said Bram, "our stage-side box awaits us."

Chapter Two

The box had luxuriously deep carpets and high backed comfortable chairs. I tried not to make a comparison with the dirty little multiplex cinemas of my day. Bram's wife, Florence, was there – a shy woman who was shocked by Lee's sharp streetwise humour that, strangely, came over as dated in these elegantly pleasant surroundings, and her sexy jokes that I had found a turn-on, now had a crude edge to them. I felt we both had to adapt to this totally different world and fast. An expectant silence from the audience brought me back from my thoughts when an off stage voice announced…'Now let our play begin'.

The mighty curtains slowly rose revealing the battlements of Elsinore Castle. I have to admit I'm not into Shakespeare, but Irving was incredible. At times, his performance was pure magic. If only it could have been captured on film for future generations. Ellen Terry played Ophelia and was equal to Henry in her style and talent. She was in turn sad, sexy, warm, and in Ophelia's mad scene, she had the audience by the throat. The brilliant costumes, huge sets and mood-setting music from the orchestra were all pure Hollywood. After the final curtain, Henry came on stage with Ellen and the other twenty members of the cast to make a short speech of thanks.

The reaction from the audience would out-do any present day rock concert. They stood, cheered, clapped, stamped and called for encore after encore so that Henry had to bring his cast on stage again and again. Lee and I were stunned by such acting – or as she put it – totally gob smacked!

"Henry would like you both to join him in the Beefsteak Room," said Bram, who could see how impressed we were.

Lee leaned back in her chair, put her hands above her head and stretched those long legs like some lazy cat. "Sure we would, Bram, where is it?"

"It is a very large room to the side of the theatre where the famous and powerful from the world over attend dinners and parties given by Henry."

The three of us made our way past men moving massive parts of scenery on small wheels and women carrying arm loads of colourful costumes. On entering this famous Beefsteak Room, we found about 150 well-heeled ones laughing and talking in loud voices about the play. Young girls, dressed as maids, were rushing about with trays full of food and drinks, while a small quartet played what sounded like waltz music.

"If this is a showbiz rave who's giving out the ecstasy? And will you look at that creep over there, does he want a smack in the mouth or what?"

I looked across the crowded room to where Lee was pointing and saw an old man clicking his fingers above his head to get the attention of one of the waitresses. "I don't think women's lib or equal rights are here yet, Lee," I said trying to calm her down.

Bram, looking surprised at Lee's reaction said, "These are the customs of our times."

Just then, an attractive smiling woman took Bram's arm saying, "I think we have a great success on our hands. This Hamlet will out-run the last one."

Turning to us, he then introduced Ellen Terry. She was tall and slim with pale blue eyes, light brown hair and very vivacious.

"What was the last Hamlet?" asked Lee.

Still smiling Ellen explained, "Henry appeared here at the Lyceum four years ago in 1874. I was not his leading lady on that occasion, but he gave a superb rendition of the Prince of Denmark, and it ran for over two hundred consecutive performances."

Fixing me with those laughing eyes she asked, "Are you Americans, you have such a strange way of speaking?"

Before I could say no, we came from right here in London, Bram jumped in with. "They come from the other side of the universe, my dear. Come, Henry is leaving and we are invited for drinks at his rooms in Mayfair. I have told him all about you." Then he added in a confiding whisper. "Well, not quite all you understand."

"We understand nothing, Bram," replied Lee. "But it sure makes a change from clubbing it in Peckham or Brixton and I'm loving it, how about you, Tel?"

"It's fascinating, so long as we can return to our own time."

"Of course you can my friends, at any time of your choosing, you just say the word. Of course, when you have seen more you may decide to stay with us and you would be most welcome."

"No chance, Bram, I'm missing my present day already."

Lee, for once, said nothing. We forced our way through the still cheering crowds towards a row of carriages and restless horses. A man opened the door of Ellen and Henry's coach and got in with them. Bram, Lee and I scrambled into the second one, then he called through the tiny window in the coach roof to the driver.

"Bond Street, my good fellow."

"As you says, gov'nor, right you are, sir," came the reply.

Lee gave me a look with raised eyebrows saying. "They think we talk strange!!"

Then winking at me she said, "Bram, at this moment in time we appear to have an ongoing situation but with some meaningful dialogue, and avoiding the worst case scenario in this milti-layered time scale – at the end of the day what's your default mode on that?"

He didn't laugh as she expected him to, but replied.

"I am aware that conversation in your time is dead. You have destroyed a once beautiful language and replaced it with meaningless analagies. Hence, you no longer understand each other."

Suitably put down we made no reply.

Lee was fascinated by the lush interior of the coach, all dark velvet and highly polished wood. As we trotted our way down the Strand towards Trafalgar Square, I noticed the lack of any high rise buildings; saw men raise their hats when greeting people; horse-drawn traffic everywhere and buses with the top deck open to the weather. We rounded a Piccadilly Circus packed with street theatre: barrel organ players with bright macaw's on their shoulders; Irish fiddlers with pet monkeys; women sitting on every kerb with bunches of flowers for sale. I heard the cry of 'who'll buy my sweet lavender'. As the coach slowed to let people cross, a young woman's face appeared at the open window demanding that I buy some London Pride for my pretty lady. I took the flowers and handed them to Lee who, most unusual for her, gave me a warm smile. In the hope of getting rid of her, I gave the woman a £10 note.

"Wot's this," she cried. "I don't want no paper, I's a poor girl I is." Then she began to sob and cry at the top of her voice.

"Here, girl," said Bram, tossing her a gold coin of some sort. She caught it quick as a flash, bit it then yelled.

"God bless yer's. You's real toffs if ever I did see 'em."

Lee called back. "Keep the tenner, your great grand kids will be able to spend it on drugs."

"Pay no attention to these riff raff," said Bram. "They can put on an act almost as well as Henry or Ellen."

We turned into Bond Street and he called once more to the coachman. "Stop on the corner of Grafton Street, at number 15A."

As we got out, I noticed how being so lightly sprung the coach tilted and swayed with our weight. Lee made a fuss of the horse, then started joking and flirting with the young coachman. The same man who I had seen get into Henry's coach opened the door to us with a polite nod of the head. Lee asked Bram if that was Henry's bodyguard.

"No," laughed Bram, "there is no need for them in this age – that's Walter Collinson, he's Henry's valet, butler, general manservant."

Lee, looking suspicious asked, "Is Henry married?"

"Oh, yes, but she is a quite impossible lady – they live apart. The truth is Henry is married to the art of acting and the Lyceum."

"Any kids?" asked Lee.

Bram, not for the first time, looked blank.

"She means any children," I explained.

"Oh! Yes, two sons, they both become actors but die tragically young: one drowns at sea with his young wife and the other dies many years before his time."

As we climbed the steep narrow stairs to Henry's apartment, it dawned on me that the shop downstairs I'd noticed with the name 'William Baldry Ltd, Drapers' is in my time 'Asprey', the high-class Mayfair jewellers. The large rooms of the apartment were furnished in dark wood except for a very decorative light satin wood piano, the lid was open and I read the makers name 'John Brinsmead & Sons, London'. Pictures hung on every wall, mainly scenes from classic plays and one large photograph of Charles Dickens taken when he was in New York. Next to that hung a long ornate sword. The windows were all stained glass, so I found the whole place rather brooding and claustrophobic. Walter served us drinks and sandwiches and then left for home. Ellen and Lee were chatting like old friends. When I tried to join in Lee snapped. "This is girl talk, so piss off."

She got away with her rudeness because those present did not understand the phrase. I thought I would try an interview with this greatest actor of all time. Studying him at close range, as opposed to seeing him fifty feet away on a stage, I would describe him as tall, thin, good looking, but with a rather grave or even sad expression. His suit was, to my eyes, old fashioned but tailor-made and finely cut. Around his neck on a silk cord hung a pair of those Pince-nez glasses that clip on the bridge of the nose. His collar length dark hair completed the image – he was every inch the bohemian actor. His manner was courteous and polite, he said nothing casually, but thought carefully before speaking in that quite melodious voice. As we discussed his early days as a struggling actor, he offered me a small cigar. As he lit his own I noticed the long thin fingers and the large signet ring.

"Tell our good friend about the ring, Henry," said Bram.

He took it off and handed it to me with great pride saying. "It once belonged to David Garrick and there is something else you must see, I have the sword once owned by Edmund Kean when he played Richard III." He sprang from the chair and went over to the wall to get it.

Bram whispered, "Garrick and Kean were the greatest Shakespearean actors before Henry's time."

As I admired the sword, he continued, "I was born in Somerset, but came to London at a very young age. My first employment was as a clerk in the city, but desperate to become an actor I took elocution lessons where one was required to read to an audience. This gave me the confidence one needs to act on stage. I went to the theatre almost every night, so knew most of the great plays by heart. My dream came true in 1856 when, in my late teens, I went on stage in the north of England, then worked in Edinburgh for three years and toured in stock companies all over the British Isles and appeared in Dublin and Paris."

As he got up to hang the sword back on the wall, Bram said quietly. "During his career he played nearly 700 different parts, including all the major Shakespearean ones and he had many plays written specially for him. He played far more parts than any actor of eminence before or since."

Settling back in his large comfortable chair, Henry seemed to be enjoying our conversation. "Another drink, my dear fellow?" he asked with a rare smile.

"Why not, Henry, I'll have a whisky," I replied. However, this sort of threw them; all that was on offer was port, brandy and wine.

"Whisky and gin are for the lower classes," laughed Ellen.

I was about to joke that you can't get much lower than Lee and me, but thought better of it and said, "I'll have a brandy, a double please." Well if you don't ask, you don't get! I don't think they understood the term double because when it came it was more like half a pint.

"So, after years in the sticks, Henry, when did you get to town?" asked Lee, who having had a few to many was becoming her usual loud self.

As if to interpret all this, Bram speaking for Henry, said. "From 1868 Henry had great successes at several London theatres, then in 1871 he starred in *The Bells* at the Lyceum, he played the part of a murderer called Mathias who is haunted by the ghost of his victim. It was one of the greatest triumphs in theatrical history. It ran for over 150 performances, and I believe even in your day, when an alarm bell sounds people will say: 'Ah! The bells!! The bells.'" In '73 he had another massive success, Eugene Aram, then in '74 the Hamlet that Ellen has already told you about, followed by Macbeth and later by Othello."

"What about a social life, Henry, how do you chill out?" asked Lee.

He must have guessed the meaning of chill out because he replied. "I have hardly any free time, but I do belong to some London clubs that are close by; The Garrick, The Green Room, The Savile."

Lee butted in loudly, "Yeah. We go clubbing a lot in Brixton. I love it, but Tel's not so keen. Can't stand the noise, the old deadbeat! I work a lotta clubs too, mainly in Soho."

"You work in clubs, whatever do you do?" asked Ellen wide eyed.

"I'm a pole dancer. It's good money. OK, I have to work nude, but I don't mind, it's fun and the pay's brilliant."

Pole dancing did not register with them, but nude did. The silence was deafening, then Ellen came to our rescue saying. "Ah, you're an artist's model, you must meet two friends of ours – Graham Robertson the artist and Johnston Forbes-Robertson, a fellow actor who is also an artist. And if you dance and sing, my dear, then we can get you work at the Gaiety Theatre."

Before she could open her big mouth again I said, "Lee, remember in this day and age gay means to be happy and cheerful."

She took the hint for once and said. "Yeah! Could you, I'd really like that, great."

The evening wore on and as I asked more questions it became clear to me that Henry was a star way beyond anyone in my time. For example, when playing *The Bells* he lived the part to such an extent that he would go white and tremble with rage and fear, and it was not unusual for him to feel such emotion on stage that he would pass out. He would do this night after night for months on end. Doctors warned him it was taking a toll on his health, but I think the man only became truly alive when on stage. The gorgeous Ellen was a different temperament, but still the greatest actress of her time. The pair made the ultimate stage partnership. And in private life? I leave that opinion to Lee who said, "I knew they were having it off as soon as I saw them, it's obvious en'it. They are in love, man – stands to reason don't it."

Bram said it was time to go and as it was gone 2am, we didn't argue. Henry, courteous as ever, kissed Lee's hand and said how much he had enjoyed our somewhat unusual conversation. Ellen told me to rap up warm because we have a pea-souper tonight. When we got to the street I realised what she meant, the fog was so thick I could not see across the street and it seemed to muffle all sound.

"The fog's are part of daily life for us, it is because everyone burns coal," laughed Bram.

A horse-drawn cab appeared through the gloom and we climbed into the cosy warmth. Bram called up to the bowler-hatted coachmen. "Lyceum Theatre, and take your time, my good man."

"I'm as good as sold, Bram," I said.

"I did not realise, sir, I had sold you anything!" he replied.

"What I mean, Bram, is I'm beginning to think you're right about Irving being the biggest star of all time. Whether he would be right for Bob's book is another matter. If only he had caught the movies."

"Ah! Yes, your moving pictures." He sighed. "Then he would be there for all time, for all to see and marvel at his Hamlet, Othello, Richelieu, Napoleon, Romeo, Richard III, Shylock, Becket, Mathias, Eugene Aram, and so many many more. In the next few years he will become one of the most famous men on earth. He will be as well known in the far western cities of America as he is in Europe, and bear in mind, my friends, that America is a far distant land, not like in your time when it can be reached in a matter of hours. We go by ship and it takes two weeks. When we get there I charter special trains to take us from city to city."

"Why do you need a train?" asked Lee.

"Because we take all the sets, scenery, costumes, around forty members of cast and some of their families and not forgetting carpenters, cooks…"

"OK, Bram, I get the picture," said Lee.

"And I might add, Madam Henry and the Lyceum Company will tour America and Canada no less than eight times in the next few years."

It was then I noticed that we were in that blue light like I'd seen in the Chrysler. "What's going on, Bram?" I asked.

"Do not fear, my friend," he replied. "To you and Miss Lee we are moving slowly in a horse and carriage, but in truth we are speeding through time and when we reach the Lyceum it will be 1895."

"Seventeen years to cover a couple of miles, that's even worse than London Transport in the rush hour! We should have gone by tube!" Lee joked. She seemed to be far more at ease with all this than me.

"Bram, do something for me. I want to prove a point to myself."

"If it is within my power, sir, I will. What is it?" he asked.

"When we get to 1882, detour down Beak Street in Soho – I live there. Next door to me there's an old pub. Up on the wall it says 'Erected 1882'."

"Come to think of it that's the last time you had an erection without my help!" said Lee almost falling off her seat, helpless with laughter.

Bram called to the driver. "Turn up Regents Street, then turn right into Beak Street."

"As you wish, sir," came the polite reply.

My street was as narrow as ever – I recognised many of the small shop fronts and alleyways, then we were outside my building, even the entrance looked much the same and on each floor instead of flats it looked like tailors' workshops. I could see men sitting cross-legged and sewing under bright gas lamps. Next-door was the pub, in the process of being built amid a mass of wooden scaffolding poles and ladders. As I gazed in disbelief, two pretty young girls came from a dark doorway up to the coach window.

"Won't it be nice when that Tavern is open, mister? You'll be able to take us ladies for a drink, still not to worry, there's one wot's open just round the corner and we'll give you a real good time." She promised, with a knowing wink of her big dark eyes. I noticed the heavy makeup and their enormous hats covered with flowers.

"Not tonight thank you, madam," answered Bram, in a firm voice.

Looking closer into the fog, I realised that women were standing in every doorway. "I am afraid London is swarming with these ladies of the night. Is it still the same in your time?" asked Bram.

Lee, who found it all highly amusing said, "The same, Bram, but very different and highly dangerous – we have AIDS that looks set to wipe us all out."

Bram told the driver to continue to the Lyceum, then turning to me asked the meaning of AIDS. "Forget it, Bram, it'll take too much explaining, but you can explain something to me – you can travel through and control time yet there are events in the future that you appear to have no knowledge of."

He thought carefully, then began slowly. "You see, my

friend, going forward or back in time is the same. For example, if you look back over the years you have lived, you cannot recall every single day. There are people and events in your life that you have totally forgotten, therefore, it follows that you can forget parts of the future."

"How come," asked Lee, showing some interest, "only you have this gift, but not Henry or Ellen?"

"I came across it quite by accident." He continued with that lilting Irish accent that gave this charming man's conversation an interesting edge. "I have a great interest in Egyptology and have a large library on the subject at home. In one of the very old books I found pages of old notes made by someone unknown years ago, written in hieroglyphics. It took me over two years to decipher them. They had been copied from inscriptions on the walls of one of the ancient tombs of the pharaohs who knew the secrets of time. I wrote *Dracula* as a play, but also wrote several books. On your return read my *The Jewel of Seven Stars*, I left clues in that book for those who can read between the lines. Alas, it would all be wasted on the people of your time."

"Why's that?" asked Lee.

"Because you have been taught to scorn the past and you certainly have no future. You're locked on the treadmill of the unending present."

"So, how far ahead can you see, Bram?"

"From where we are now, about two hundred years and yes, before you ask, I know how you both will die, but I have grown far too fond of you to ever reveal it, so don't even ask me."

He said it almost casually as he looked out of the carriage window at the swirling fog. Lee and I said nothing, but we both sensed that Bram did not like what he saw. In the silence, Lee lent over, gave me a gentle kiss and put her hand protectively over mine. But in the coach there was now an eerie chill, a weird sense of doom.

"We're here," Lee shouted, "back at the dear old Lyceum. Fill us in Bram, what year does your pocket watch have?"

"Yes, before we alight," said Bram, "it is the afternoon of Thursday, 19th July and the year is 1895. Yesterday, Henry was called to Windsor Castle where Her Majesty Queen Victoria knighted him. He is the first actor ever to receive this honour – the whole nation is rejoicing. Sir Henry is now at the zenith of his career, never was a person of the theatre so loved by the public and indeed his fellow players, as you're about to see, my friends. Follow me if you will."

The fog had gone, now it was a warm sunny day with a brilliant blue sky above. A large notice outside said 'Theatre closed for one day only'.

"Let us in on it, Bram, what's the occasion?" asked Lee.

"To celebrate Henry being knighted, his fellow actors and friends are going to make a presentation to him because he has brought great honour to this profession, you might say he has made us all respectable." Bram gave a rare laugh then continued. "There are well over 4000 people here today plus music, good food, drink and the rich and famous from every walk of life. So, mix and enjoy yourselves and think no more about what I told you in the coach."

Easier said than done, I thought as I took Lee in my arms and moved onto the small dance floor in front of the stage. It was good to hold her again. It always gave me a thrill to be close to her; for me she had that magic that comes along only once; and she could hold her own with the women dancing close by and there were some real beauties. The women of this age are feminine; their dresses, hats, hairstyles, all give them terrific sex appeal. In my mind's eye, I saw the women at my local supermarket with their worn down trainers, baggy jeans and T-shirts covered in silly slogans. Maybe I should take Bram's advice and not return to my own time. Lee whispered in my ear. "Have you told me the truth about your age – how come you do this old fashioned dancing so well?"

Before I could answer, Bram took my arm and leading us through the crowd of happy excited people said, "Come, I want to show both of you the great stars of my day; their names are known and admired throughout the world."

We wound our way through the 4000 strong crowd of celebrities to the edge of the auditorium to get a better view of this astonishing day in the history of showbiz. Tables were laden with food and drink; a small orchestra played Gilbert and Sullivan and there was an air of happy excitement that even Lee and I could tune into. I realised that we had not been this happy and relaxed in ages. "I have to tell you, Bram," I said, "I don't recognise any of these world famous, never to be forgotten people!" I never meant it to, but my casual remark hurt him – he looked sad, so I quickly added. "But I bet I'll know their names, point some out to me."

"I will indeed," he replied slowly. "Fame is such a fleeting thing. You own the world one day, you're forgotten the next. This is especially true in your dreadful times. Your moving pictures, your music, if from only a few years before, are laughed at and worse still despised! The only lasting art form is books; they have a curious way of surviving."

Just then the Lyceum erupted into rapturous applause – Irving had arrived! He strode in, a tall gaunt figure in a long black coat and black silk hat with a wide brim, at his heels a small dog.

"What's with the dog?" asked Lee.

"That's Fussie," said Bram. "He is Henry's faithful

companion of many years, his beloved Fox Terrier goes everywhere with him."

"Looks like a Jack Russell to me," replied Lee.

Bram continued. "The elderly man with Henry is a lifelong friend, John Toole, the greatest comedian of the age. He has his own theatre just across the road; no longer there in your time, of course."

As Irving made his way to the stage, he stopped often to have a pleasant word with everyone. When he got to us, I could see the strain of the years in his still handsome face. "You won't recall me, Sir Henry," I said. "We met way back in 78. I just want to say congratulations."

He looked at Lee and me with a puzzled expression, and then said, "I do, indeed, recall you sir, and thank you. If I may say so, the years have been deuced kind to both of you, upon my word, you don't look a day older! You must know the secrets of Mr Wilde's 'Dorian Gray.'" Before moving on he shook my hand and as he did so, I noticed he still wore the ring that bore the miniature picture of Shakespeare that he'd shown us that night at his flat.

"You must visit Ellen and I. Bram will arrange it. I look forward to some more interesting conversation, God bless you both."

"That's what I call one hell of a personality," said Lee, as

Irving's tall figure moved on through the adoring crowd. "Who are the two sulky looking gits standing away from the rest over there?" asked Lee, pointing to a thin man with whiskers.

"I regret to say," said Bram, "he is a fellow countryman of mine called George Bernard Shaw, known to one and all as GBS. He is a playwright and journalist and in love with Ellen Terry, who for some silly reason strings him along. Anyway, he hates and loathes Henry and whenever he can write something nasty about him, he does."

I just knew Lee wouldn't let that pass and she didn't disappoint me saying, "So Ellen likes to prick tease the stupid sod who can't get the message that he stands no chance against Henry. I think GBS needs some GBH!!"

"And the other man?" I asked quickly.

Bram sighed and said, "That's a friend of GBS who also has an intense dislike and jealousy of Henry, name's William Archer. He's a drama critic, writes for a magazine called *The World*."

"Wow!" squealed Lee. "I've gotta know who's the dish with all the birds around him"

Bram, by now, was getting the hang of our slang. "Ah!" said Bram, with a smile. "That is William Terriss. He worked with Henry for years and toured America with him. They are great friends, but he became too big a star to be in anyone's shadow, so he and his leading lady (and between ourselves lover) Jessie Millward took over the Adelphi Theatre in the Strand, where they do what is known as melodramas. After Henry and Ellen, they are the most famous couple in London."

"Are his wife and lover here tonight, Bram?"

"Yes, indeed," said Bram. "And that very lovely young girl next to him is Ellaline Terriss, his daughter. She will, when those around us tonight have begun our journey into eternity, become London's biggest musical star of the Edwardian era through to the 1940's."

"Maybe so," said Lee, "but I'm gonna pull that guy. He's too good too miss! I'll give him a chat-up line he can't resist!" With that she made a beeline for Terriss. Two minutes after that, she was holding him close on the dance floor. Bram gave me a look of shock-horror.

"Don't worry, I'm used to it." I laughed. "Show me some more famous ones."

He looked around then said, "Ah! You see the two gentlemen deep in conversation up in the gallery; I suspect they are still known in your time, the one who looks agitated because he is very highly strung is Hall Caine, the most popular writer of our time and a great friend of Henry's. He has travelled over from the Isle of Man where he lives." I told Bram his book sales must have dried up, I'd not heard of him, then asked who the other guy was.

"Walter Sickert, the artist," answered Bram.

Obviously surprised that I didn't recognise him. "Sorry, Bram, his name also means nothing in my time."

"Well it might when I tell you more." He continued. "Many years ago, he tried his hand at being an actor and got a few walk-on parts at the Lyceum, but the man had no talent for it and Henry advised him to try something else, so he studied art and has become very successful. About seven years ago, if memory serves me well it was August 1888, Jekyll and Hyde opened here at the Lyceum and Sickert came every night, always alone. He was obsessed by the play and it was exactly that time the brutal murders started of poor down and out women in the East End. Sickert knew those women. He was also a friend of the royal family, especially Prince Eddy, son of the Prince of Wales, who he introduced to these women for, shall we say, sexual purposes. One of them – Mary Kelly, a prostitute – tried to blackmail the Prince about a baby girl called Alice, born to one of the women claiming the Prince was the father! If this were made public it would cause a revolution, so Sickert, on orders from above, murdered them all including Mary. Since then he appears to have become very wealthy! In your time he is known as 'Jack the Ripper.'"

"That, Bram, is incredible!" I replied. "Yes, old 'Jack' is still big news in my time. When I return I'll have the answer to a crime that's intrigued people for well over a century, could make me wealthy!"

Bram laughed and said, "We must change the subject to one more pleasant. You see the dark, rather shy looking lady there by the orchestra, that's Ada Rehan, a very popular Irish-American actress. She is just as famous and loved by the public as Ellen Terry yet, sadly, her nerves and shyness will wear her down and in a few short years she will die lonely and forgotten back in America. The lively lady talking to her is 'Our Nellie', Nellie Farran, the Queen of the Gaiety Theatre – what you would call musical comedy. She sings, dances, and tells jokes. The working classes worship her. She too had a marvellous stage partner called Fred Leslie, but he caught typhoid and was dead at only 37. That was three years ago, but the brave lady carries on and her theatre is sold out every night."

"As we put it, Bram," I said, "she puts bums on seats. What becomes of her?"

"Already arthritis is slowing her career. Within a year she will be in a wheel chair never able to appear on stage again. The very handsome young lad over there is Gordon Craig, Ellen Terry's son, soon to become a great actor. He works with and idolises Irving, and when Irving dies he is devastated and never acts again, goes to live in Italy. In 1966, aged 96, as he dies his last words will be 'look Fussie has jumped on the bed and here's Henry. Oh! It's so good to see you both, I knew you'd come for me.'"

"Fascinating stuff, Bram," I said, "but I have to tell you that none of these people have stood the test of time."

"What about Oscar Wilde?"

"His name is still known, if only as a gay icon."

"Yes," replied Bram, "he is the most witty and amusing chap."

I let Bram's failure to grasp modern words pass – it would take too much explaining.

"Oscar," he continued, "must long to be here tonight, but he's a homosexual so they locked the poor devil away in prison just a few weeks ago, on 25th May, for two long years."

"The only name I know that's really lasted is yours," I told him. He stared at me in stunned silence then said slowly.

"Whatever do you mean?" Then I remembered he'd told me there were large parts of the future he did not know about or, as he put it, he had forgotten. "There are a couple of seats by that table, can we sit down?" he asked.

Once sitting quietly I tried to explain to him. "If your name is mentioned in my day you'll get the answer 'Oh! The man who wrote *Dracula*,' not the man who ran the Lyceum for Henry

Irving. You're far better known than Henry or Ellen or just about anyone I can think of from this era!"

His voice had dropped to a whisper as he said, "But you, sir, when we met you said you had not read my book."

"That's right. A story about a man dressed in a black cloak going around sinking his fangs into the necks of pretty girls is not my scene; but it must be the scene for millions of others. Remember, there are so many types of entertainment in my day and your work is on all of them; TV, movies, radio, video and DVD. That, as you call it 'magic box' that Lee carried, what I call a laptop, has all the answers to any question you care to ask. Well, last night I asked about Bram Stoker and it told me your book *Dracula* has never been out of print since the day you wrote it! It's been translated into every language. In fact, the only book to out-sell it is the Bible!! Your other books have been steady sellers too. Your sales must be hundreds of millions! You definitely have cult status. Come back with me and I guarantee you fame and fortune."

I knew he didn't understand all I'd told him, but he got the drift of it. He sat still and staring in front of him at the noisy happy mass of people, but not seeing them because tears filled his eyes, then he spoke slowly. "So, I have entertained more people than all these great and talented ones here tonight?"

"This lot multiplied by millions," I replied.

"You cannot possibly know, dear friend, what it means to me to know this," he said. "What you tell me makes all the loneliness, struggle and hard work worthwhile."

It dawned on me that no one had paid any attention to this big man sitting here crying. I was starting to realise people of this time show their emotions much more freely, even the paper boy when we entered the theatre was laughing and joking as he handed out the news, and men whistled a happy tune as they walked along the street. What the hell for I wondered. Their faces did not have the crafty, suspicious, aggressive expressions that I see everyday on the streets of London.

Deafening cheers and applause broke my thoughts. Up on the stage, speeches had been made and they were presenting Henry with what looked like a glass sided casket and a huge book. Henry was overcome with emotion; even this was received with tumultuous enthusiasm from his audience, who were as highly charged as he was. He made a charming speech of thanks and sat down, looking stunned by the sheer love shown to him this afternoon by his profession and the people of London.

Lee had joined us full of stories about 'Breezy Bill' (the nick name for William Terriss) and all the big names he had introduced her to. Like everyone else we made our way onto the stage to see at close hand what Henry had been given. The eager crowd gathered round the table to see a large rectangular casket in gold and crystal. Bram, seeing how impressed Lee and I were explained. "The design is classical, twelve fluted columns in the Ionic order, all solid gold. It is a beautiful specimen of the English goldsmith's art and contains over one hundred ounces of eighteen-carat gold. On the front panel, also in gold, are the masks of 'Tragedy' and 'Comedy'. His friend, the actor and artist, Mr Forbes Robertson designed it."

Lee leant over and read aloud the enamelled inscription. "This casket was presented with the address which it encloses, by the actors and actresses of Great Britain and Ireland, to Sir Henry Irving to commemorate the Knighthood conferred upon him by her Majesty Queen Victoria. MDCCCXCV. Wow!" shouted Lee, causing those nearby to look over at us in surprise then she said, "That is really something and just take a look at this huge book. Tell us about it, Bram."

"Well, my dear, it is a testimonial to the affection in which we all hold Sir Henry. It has 400 leaves of pure vellum; these have been signed by over 4000 of his friends and fellow artists. The leaves, or pages as you would call them, are decorated in gold and it is bound in Levant morocco."

"Well!" laughed Lee. "We did want to know the most loved actor of all time and I guess we found him. Don't Henry and Ellen look happy with all their friends around them, makes me feel all sort of romantic," she sighed, with a dreamy look in her sparkling blue eyes.

"You're present, my friends, at the very peak of Henry's fame," said Bram, taking in the incredible scene. "His talent, his fellow artists, his adoring public will stay with him to the end but, alas, the gods will turn against him as they always do. In a few weeks, he and the whole Lyceum Company will start another American tour that will be, yet again, a great success, but trouble and tragedy lay in wait for him on his return; yet being the man he is he will…go forth to meet the shadowy future without fear, and with a manly heart."

Bram Stoker.

Henry Irving in 1878.

Ellen Terry.

Henry as Hamlet and Ellen as Ophelia at the Lyceum in 1878.

Nellie Farren, superstar of the 1890s. At her funeral service in 1905 (Lee) – Letty Lind, made a short speech saying what a doll Nellie was and she was now in the land of the moonlight shadows!! Next day the press asked what language was she speaking?

Henry learning a new part at his flat in Grafton Street, Mayfair.

William Terriss and Jessie Millward on stage at the Adelphi in 1887.
Insert: Ivor Novello at The Adelphi in 1944 at the 1897th performance of
'Dancing Years'.

Top: The circle and boxes, Lyceum, 1895.

Below: The columns outside the Lyceum draped in black
after Irvings death in 1905.

The Lyceum in 1939 when Pad took his photos.

Top: Henry with his dog 'Fussie'.

Below: Henry and Bram leaving the stagedoor of the Lyceum.

Interior and exterior of the Lyceum, 1895.

Henry in later years.

Ellen in later years.

Henry's room's in Grafton Street, Mayfair as they look today
where he lived for 27 years.

The Dog's Cemetery in Hyde Park where Henry had 'Fussie',
his much loved Terrier buried.

MY GENTLE LITTLE FRIEND
AND COMPANION FOR 11 YEARS
SO SADLY MISSED

SLEEP LITTLE ONE SLEEP
REST GENTLY THY HEAD
AS EVER THOU DIDST AT MY FEET
AND DREAM THAT I AM ANEAR

I FAITHFULLY LOVED AND CARED
FOR YOU LIVING. I THINK WE
SHALL SURELY MEET AGAIN

The priceless gold casket and book presented to Irving on his
Knighthood in 1895. In 1907 Letty Lind borrowed it to put on show at
the Theatre. While in her care – it disappeared! Letty (Lee), was said to
be distraught – although later that year she purchased a fabulously
expensive motor yacht moored in Monte Carlo.

This photo was taken a few months ago in a Soho club – it's Lee about to start her striptease act. An identical photo in a 1901 Gaiety Theatre program states it's Letty Lind.

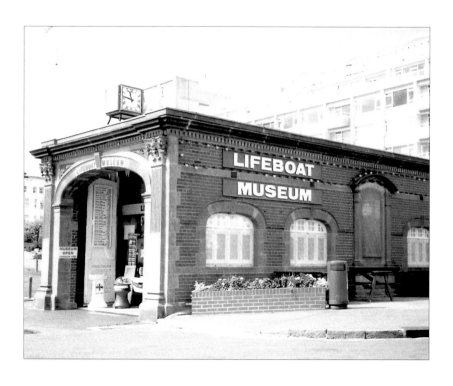

This museum erected in memory of William Terriss
stands today on the beach at Eastbourne, Sussex.

The statue of Henry Irving stands at the end of Irving Street
in London's West End, less than a mile from his Lyceum.
In December 1910 a crowd of 2000 people attended the unveiling
ceremony. Among the many famous invited guests were Mr Bram
Stoker who escorted Miss Letty Lind.

In 1880 Onslow Ford produced this lifesize marble statue of
Henry Irving as Hamlet. Ford died young but as a result of this
statue he is regarded as one of the greatest sculptor's of all time.
Bram said he got Henry's face and hands exactly true to life.
Today it stands in the Guidhall in London.

Ellaline Terriss (daughter of William) who, with help from
Henry and Ellen, became a superstar of the Edwardian era
following her father's murder.

The alleyway (as it is today) that run's alongside
the Adelphi Theatre where William Terriss was stabbed to death
as he entered the private stagedoor.

Richard Prince, the man who stabbed actor William Terriss to death
outside the stagedoor of the Adelphi Theatre.

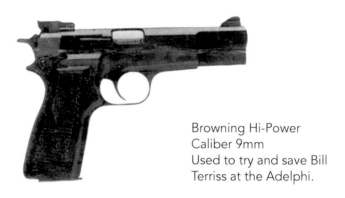

Browning Hi-Power
Caliber 9mm
Used to try and save Bill
Terriss at the Adelphi.

Smith & Wesson 36
Caliber .38mm
Used by Lee on
Waterloo Bridge.

Walther P.38
Caliber 9mm
Used by Ben on the
London Underground Train

My Chrysler C-300 that Lee loved to drive – the number plate was her idea. Photo taken before it got struck by lightening!!

The supercharged Railton that Delroy lent me.
Seen here parked just outside Winchelsea.

Ellen Terry's house at Smallhythe in Kent where she died in 1928.
Today it is the Ellen terry Museum.

The painting by Kath's mother which she gave to Lee in 1901
of Ellen Terry's house in Winchelsea.

Ellen Terry's house as it is today.

(Kath) – Katherina Forbes-Dunlop pictured at her home in Winchelsea.
As a child she and her sister were almost run down by Irving who was
driving Ellen's horse and carriage too fast.

(Lee) – Letty Lind, star of the Gaiety Theatre, 1901.
Picture taken from Kath's book.

Chapter Three

Once more, on leaving the Lyceum, the three of us were shrouded in that now familiar soft blue light. It reminded me of the low light they have at night in the intensive care ward in hospitals. We came through the light to find ourselves in a large comfortable room, furnished in dark wood with a great many indoor plants. Reading my thoughts as ever Bram said, "We have moved forward only two years to 1897, it is noon on Thursday, 16th December and we are about to enjoy a meal at my house in Chelsea." Just then his wife and son joined us and at the same time two maids brought in trays of food and best of all a silver tea service.

"About time, I'm dying for a cuppa!" said Lee.

"You have already met my dear wife, but permit me to introduce my son. This is Noel," said Bram, proudly.

I shook hands with a young man of about 18. I could tell he was taken with Lee. Even if he couldn't make out what she was on about it was plain he enjoyed the body language. After the meal, while Lee held the attention of Bram's wife and son with one of her crazy stories, I asked Bram why we were here at this date and time and what event in Henry's life were we about to witness.

"I am really not quite sure," he said to my surprise, then

continued. "As I told you, I forget parts of the future just as when you look back over your life there are large parts or events that you have forgotten, or at least you need some clue to help you recall them clearly. For example, I can tell you in detail about the real reasons for the two devastatingly evil world wars that will happen in the first half of the next century, but I know little of the years between those wars."

"Yes, I understand," I said. That was a total lie. I believed it, was utterly fascinated by it, petrified of it – yes; but understood it – never. No way would I ever get my head around this one.

I should have known my lie would be found out because he read my thoughts, smiling at me he said, "Think about this, my friend. Take the simple calculation one divided by zero, it cannot be quantified by the human mind or even by Lee's magic box; mathematicians think an answer exists and they call it infinity. I am sure you will agree this proves the existence of concepts that are beyond our comprehension and cannot be measured scientifically."

"Yeah. I agree, Bram. At least I think I do." Then, for some unknown reason I asked him. "Is there a God, Bram?"

"Yes, my friend, there is," he answered me without a moment's hesitation then added. "Nothing we can conceive of can be greater than God. There can be no faith without risk.

The existence of God cannot be proved, only believed."

I couldn't think of a suitable reply, so we sat in silence for several minutes, Bram staring into the distance as though seeing and hearing things hidden from Lee and myself. His wife and son had now left the room; she said they had to visit someone, but I suspect she feared for her son's safety with Lee giving him the full blast of her sexual charms!

"Stop daydreaming, Bram, and tell us why we're here in '97," said Lee.

He gave her a blank stare then seemed to come back to us saying, "I may have made a slight miscalculation, perhaps we should have been here last Saturday, on the 11th."

"Why, what was going down then?" she asked.

"Henry , for all his fame, is essentially a lonely man and he loved his dog Fussie so much that it occurred to me at times he loved it more than any human. Last Saturday, he was appearing at the Theatre Royal, Manchester and during rehearsals the dog fell 30 feet through a trap door on the stage and was killed instantly. Henry took the dog in his arms and went back to the hotel. When Ellen went to see him she found him talking to Fussie, who he had laid on a chair as though he was still alive. It was Ellen who gave him the dog many years before; it even travelled to America with him. Henry had it buried in The Dogs Cemetery in Hyde Park."

"I've never heard of a cemetery in Hyde Park," I said.

"Yes, indeed," he replied. "It is a railed off section on the right as you come through Lancaster Gate. There are rows of tombstones erected to departed pets. I can quote you the inscription on the headstone that Henry wrote himself. Would you like to hear it?"

"Yeah, why not. Let's have it," said Lee.

Bram gave a slight cough and began. "In loving memory of Fussie. My gentle little friend and companion, so sadly missed. Sleep little one, sleep. Rest gently thy head. As ever thou didst at my feet. And dream that I am near. I faithfully loved and cared for you living. I think we shall surely meet again." Bram paused, then said, "Of course, such sentiment would not be tolerated in your age. Sentimentality is regarded in your time as a sin. Yet I feel that cemetery proves the fact, upheld by all who love animals that their friendship can be more rewarding and more sadly missed than human friends often are, but as I say it was a major blow for Henry."

"If he was around in our day he'd be a member of Animals Rights," laughed Lee.

"Even so," said Bram, "I feel we are here on the 16th for another reason." Then getting out of his chair quickly, he said, "Come with me to the library."

Once there, we were confronted with rows of large heavy

old books.

"You don't go in for paperbacks do you, Bram?" laughed Lee, looking around at the packed shelves.

"I study astrology as well as Egyptology. I often combine the two to solve a time problem." He got down a couple of big books and began flicking through the pages as fast as he could.

I noticed beads of sweat on his forehead; and as he ran his finger down the lines on the page his hand was trembling.

"Ah! Yes, yes. I knew something was not as it should be. There must be a reason for us being here today and it is a serious one; evil is closing in on Henry or someone close to him and closing fast, my friends! What's the star sign for this month?" He asked the question as though talking to himself.

"22nd November to 21st December is Sagittarius," said Lee, looking anxiously at me.

"No. No, my dear, I work on the Egyptian horoscope devised by the ancient pharaohs and finished in the time of Cleopatra," answered Bram, getting more and more agitated. "Each of the twelve signs is ruled by an Egyptian god. It was discovered on the ceiling in the Temple of Hathor at Dendera in central Egypt. Ah! Here it is," said Bram, not taking his eyes from the page. "Oh no! We are in the time of the God 'Sekhmet' who rules from 27th November to 26th December."

Bram grabbed a paper and pencil and began working out some sort of chart. Lee took a credit card sized calculator from her pocket saying, "You call out the figures, Bram, I'll give you the answers."

He began asking Lee to subtract this by multiplying that. It was above my head, but I could see he had gone white so I went to his drinks cabinet and poured a couple of large brandies.

"And what about me, you prat?" Lee shouted.

"Sorry, I wasn't thinking," I said, pouring a third.

"I have a bearing," said Bram gravely, who was now using some sort of a slide rule and asking Lee to work out figures based on the speed of light. "I was off course," said Bram, "but only by a few hundred yards. The forces of evil are not heading for Henry's Lyceum; they're speeding across time to the Adelphi! A man will survive or be doomed."

Bram was now seated at the table with his head in his hands, eyes closed and shaking with emotion. "I hear a noise, an awful wailing, like a siren – there is fear in the air." He spoke so quietly we could hardly hear him. He went on, "If we can get this man through tonight we have saved him." Then writing furiously and asking Lee for mathematical answers at the same time he said, "I have a date; Tuesday, 20th June 1944."

"What the hell has that got to do with the Irving era?" I asked.

"Now I have a name; Ivor Novello and The Dancing Years."

"Bram are you winding us up. What the shit are you on?" screamed Lee.

Bram held up his hands as if to say, 'I just don't know.' Then he said quietly, "Does it mean anything to you, my friends?"

"For Christ's sake, Bram, 1944 was about sixty years before our time."

"Wait! Wait!" I said, "It rings a bell."

"Oh! Come on, Tel, you don't remember this Novello."

"No, but my Gran was a great fan, always talking about him, he got put in nick during the war. Petrol was on ration and his driver got some on the side, so they banged him up for six months for something he hadn't done! He was a genius; wrote the shows, the music, played the leading parts, you name it. A real superstar. Even played Hamlet! That date you mention must be his return to the stage after prison. My Gran told us he expected to be booed off the stage, but he got a great reception. The public loved him. Gran was there, she said the danger had passed, he was back where he belonged: a superstar. And she told us there was an air raid warning during the show telling people to take cover, but nobody left the Adelphi. That noise you heard must have been the siren."

Bram looked at me and said, "Give my thanks to your grandmother, I have a hunch it could be Terriss."

"Bill! Why, Bram?" asked Lee.

"They are almost the same age, both played Shakespeare, both handsome and loved by the ladies. In fact, they look very similar and both starred at the Adelphi. I was close; you may not think so, but only 47 years out when working in millions. Now I should be able to prove it." He began writing down figures again. I poured more brandies – three this time. "1897, it is 1897, my god that's it. Added together comes to 25; too much to explain and no time. Trust me, my friends; come with me with your modern ways of violence. You may be able to change history."

We rushed down the stairs into the street. On a wall I saw Durham Place, SW3; so that's where we are. A hansom cab was parked at the end of the street. Bram handed the driver some gold coins saying, "The Strand, Adelphi Theatre and drive like the wind."

"Me and old Lucy 'ere will do our best, gov'nor, I promise yer," said the old coachman.

With no roundabouts, traffic lights, zebras or one-ways to cope with the cab thundered along at break neck speed. Bram, holding a strap to stop himself being flung from side to side began to breathlessly explain. "You see, the final part of the puzzle was the age of the man who is in danger. My calculations told me his age must be 50. Now, at that time of dreadful crisis for Novello at the Adelphi in 1944 he was 51. You see, I arrive at the age by adding the figures of our year 1897 together."

"Bram, darling," said Lee, "I hate to tell you, but I must, before the mad cowboy driving this four wheeled go-cart slams us into a wall. The answer to that sum comes to 25! And neither one of those two men will see 25 again. Now, can we slow down for Christ's sake?"

Bram, shouting to make himself heard above the sound of galloping hooves and the clatter of steel rimmed wheels on a rough road replied, "True, my dear Miss Lee, but I have to double that figure because there are two 1897s in the equation; the present year, of course, and the fact that when Ivor Novello stepped onto the Adelphi stage, that night in June 1944, it was exactly the 1,897th performance of Dancing Years."

"OK, don't tell me," said Lee sadly, "that makes 50 and Bill Terriss is 50, right?"

"Yes, my dear, he is and is appearing tonight in a drama with Jessie Millward called Secret Service."

By now we had rounded Hyde Park Corner and were racing flat out along Piccadilly. "What else did your Egyptian gods show you, Bram?" I asked, scared of what the answer might be.

"I see a man's arm raised holding a large butcher's knife and it being plunged into our defenceless friend, William Terriss, three times."

In times of danger I've noticed that Lee becomes ice cool, not to mention ruthless. A couple of weeks ago in Oxford Street, carjackers tried to grab the Chrysler while she was at the wheel, she hit the one who came to the door with a spray of gas. As he staggered back holding his face she then drove into him knocking him aside. Smashed legs and broken back would be the least he got away with!

"Where is Bill now, Bram?" she asked.

"He is moving parallel with us in time towards the Adelphi, but at a much slower rate; he is nearer so will arrive at the stage door a few minutes after 7.00pm." Bram seemed to sense that if anyone could alter history Lee could.

"Right, Tel, what time is it?" I pressed the button on my talking wristwatch, an oriental girl's voice said: "The time is 6.48 and 10 seconds."

Bram looked astounded then said, "My friends, you live in an age of terrifying magic."

Lee put her face close to mine and said in a slow deliberate voice. "You fuck me and often. But don't fuck with me, OK! I know you're carrying a gun, don't give me any crap lies, we don't have the time. You made a big show about me and my gas spray when I thought Bram was a mugger outside the Lyceum, but I know when we went to that last Brixton party my pal Delroy, who has the car repair shop, sold you a gun because I heard him offer to show you how to use it out in the yard and you told him no need because you'd been in the army and knew how to use one."

"Lee, I live in Soho, it's crawling with crack heads and muggers, I need protection." I told her. She'd caught me off guard; I'd no idea the crafty bitch knew about my carrying a gun. I had no licence, so if caught I'd get five years. It's a Browning Hi-Power 9mm, a few years old, but well made and very accurate, at close or medium range it kills, further away than that it will still put a man down! "Anyway, why do you ask?" I said defensively.

"Promise me you'll shoot this bastard before he can harm Bill."

I looked into her eyes and thought of all those nights and said, "Yes, I promise, but just for the record I noticed you went missing with Terriss the other night at the Lyceum."

She gave that innocent big-eyed look and said, "Yeah! So what. I fancied him like crazy; you know I go for older men. I found a quiet room and had my legs wrapped around him in no time!"

The horse's legs were skidding as the old driver tried to stop the lurching cab. The poor beast looked like a dragon snorting fire with clouds of hot breath coming from its nostrils. We'd come to a stop just past the Adelphi. Lee jumped clear; I followed and heard Bram behind me tell the driver to wait. The pavement was crowded with theatregoers. It was getting dark and we were looking for a murderous nutter, with no idea what he looked like. Lee had the gas spray in her hand as we raced to the main entrance.

"No!" Shouted Bram. "You want the stage door just round the corner on the right, that's where Bill will enter the theatre."

I pulled my gun and slipped off the safety catch. "Lee," I shouted. "I'll stay here by the stage door, you stand out on the Strand. If he gets past you, I'll drop him before he gets to Bill."

I saw her looking frantically up and down the Strand for Bill's cab. Everyone that passed me I studied closely. Only one guy caught my attention because he was cross-eyed and looked tired and weak. Just another dirty dosser I thought. Anyway, he'd continued past up the alley.

"What time is it?" yelled Lee.

"Dead on seven." I called back. I could see her talking to Bram, then suddenly, I saw him put his hand to his heart in shock and say something to her.

She turned like lightning and sprinted towards me. As she flew past she yelled, "Bram's just said there's another private entrance in Maiden Lane, at the top of this alley. Bill could be arriving there."

I took off after her, then events went into slow motion, my brain took in about ten things at the same time. First, I saw a guy paying the driver of a hansom cab (this later turned out to be Bill's pal Henry Graves). Bill was bending, putting a key into a lock, at the same time I saw the dirty dosser coming up fast behind Bill's back with a knife! Lee, who was well in front of me, screamed and fired the gas, but she wasn't close enough for it to have any effect. I stopped running, rested the barrel of the Browning on my left forearm and took aim, but Lee was in my line of fire, then a second later she'd moved to the left and I saw the nutter plunging the knife into Bill's back. As Bill turned in shock, he knifed him again in the chest, at the same time I fired twice and the first bullet hit the knife blade and smashed it out of his hand, the second hit the wall inches from him then ricocheted gashing his head. With blood pouring from the wound he stumbled away, but Lee caught up with him. As he cowered against the wall she fired the gas directly into his face. He started coughing and choking; like his lungs were on fire and with traces of blood seeping from his tight shut eyes he sank to the ground.

Screaming, "You bastard." Lee then kicked him hard and repeatedly in the bollocks. Turning to me she said, "Give me the gun, I'll shove it in his gob and blow his face in half."

Between spasms of choking, the nutter gasped, "Spare me, I've not eaten in three days."

"Kill the bastard, Tel, kill him!" screamed Lee.

"OK. OK, I'll finish him. You get back to Bill. He needs you." I told her. With that she tore off back to where Bill was slumped against the doorway and took him in her arms. I pressed my gun against the side of the nutter's head. He began to shake violently. I asked his name.

"Richard Prince, sir. I am an actor. Finish me, sir. Finish me. I beg you."

He had a strong Scots accent, was about forty with a heavy moustache. I noticed his coat – it was old and torn; on his feet he wore boots with the sole worn through and no socks on his dirty feet. Maybe as a last try for style he had around his neck an old worn red cravat! He was now flat on the ground and trying to slowly drag himself away from me. In God's name, what am I doing, I asked myself. I had no right to kill this pathetic arsehole! I put the safety catch back on and put the gun back in my inside pocket. Whistles were blowing and police with high button tunics were running in from the Strand. Someone said a doctor was on his way from Charing Cross Hospital.

Getting back to Lee I saw that another woman was now

holding Bill. It was Jessie Millward, his partner, who had got to the theatre early.

"Come, my friends, we can do nothing more." said Bram, softly.

With that, Bill reached out a hand to me weakly. It felt like ice. As I held it he said, "Goodbye, my friends, you tried to save me. I realise now where you come from. God bless you both." As I turned to go I heard him say to Jessie. "Sis, I am stabbed."

We drove slowly back in the same cab. I put my arms round Lee as tears streamed down her face. "I guess you're ashamed of us, Bram. You must think we're wild animals," I said, avoiding his eyes and looking out of the window.

"I have no right to judge those who are forced to live by other rules than I. Anyway, it was my fault, I forgot the private entrance. It was built for the Queen so she can enter the theatre unnoticed," he said, then added. "Your time is a truly god forsaken one. You're good people ruled by the forces of evil."

"What was the outcome back there?" I asked him.

"Prince will spend the rest of his life in Broadmoor, a criminal lunatic asylum. He will die there in 1937. In his deranged mind, he thought Terriss should give him a leading role at the Adelphi. 50,000 people will line the route of Bill's funeral – all the way to the Brompton Cemetery. Sir Henry will escort Jessie. The whole country will go into mourning. He was a much-loved entertainer and a keen sailor, so the public will donate money for a new lifeboat house to be built in his memory on the beach at Eastbourne. I think you will find it still there in your time."

"That's nice. He'd like that. He told me he had a boat," said Lee, drying her tears.

"Tell me something, Miss Lee. Why do you wear that gold cobra bracelet?" asked Bram.

"It was a present from the gunman here, for being, shall we say, very naughty!" She laughed loudly. I thought how quickly the tears had stopped.

"What made you choose it, sir?"

"I didn't, Bram. Lee did, I only paid for it! To be honest, I don't like it. Strange, but it makes me feel uneasy."

"Not strange at all, sir. The sign of the Cobra Queen should put the fear of God into you!"

Before I could ask what he meant, the coach was jolting to a stop; we were back at his place. As we got out he gave the coachman another gold coin saying, "Well done, my good man."

"Cor blimey, gov'nor," said the old man. "You's a gent an' no mistake! Thanks to you, me and old Lucy 'ere will have a few days rest! God bless yer all."

Bram put the heavy books back on the shelves in the library, and all the papers with his calculations on them back in the drawer, then poured me a drink and told a maid to bring us a snack.

"So. We can't change history, Bram," I said.

"Oh! Yes, indeed, it is possible. You see there are countless parallel lifetimes running alongside ours; in one of those your bullet hit Prince so you saved the life of Terriss."

"Then I could have had him and ended up a Victorian superstar," said Lee tactlessly, then continued, "So, poor Henry lost his little dog that meant so much to him, now his best mate's been murdered!"

"My studies in such matters show that tragic events occur in sequences of three, so a third one for Henry is close – do you wish to witness it?"

"Sure, why not," said Lee. "Who knows, we may be able to change history even if it's only in some other lifetime."

"We have only to move forward about eight weeks to the early hours of Friday, 18th February 1898, and, although nothing in this room has changed we are now at that time, so finish your drinks my violent, but likeable, friends."

No sooner had Bram finished speaking when there came a loud banging on his street door. I pressed my watch, the oriental girl told me it was 5.10 am.

"Let's go," shouted Lee, as she ran down the stairs ahead of me and Bram.

A cab driver, who looked like he was freezing, handed Bram a note. He read it quickly then said, "It's from the police, I am wanted at Bear Lane, Southwark immediately!"

We piled in again, this time it was a big four-wheeler, so we have more room and we have two-horse power! It crossed my mind as we tore-arsed through the streets once again that this was more Wild West Wells Fargo then the grid locked West End I knew.

"Bram, I can't see you and Henry going south of the river; what's down in Southwark for the likes of you blokes? Are you slumming it?" asked Lee.

"The note told me of a fire, my dear. It can only mean one thing; the scenery for all our Lyceum productions is on fire! You see, we rent two huge railway arches from the Southern Railway Company down there and store tonnes and tonnes of drapes, sets, scenery and theatrical equipment of all kinds."

At Ludgate Circus, the driver was not sure of the way, so it was my turn to call through the small roof window. "Cut down over Blackfriars Bridge then go left into Southwark Street and it's on the right." Bram looked at me in surprise, so I said, "We're 'Sarf Londoners', we go drinking in that part of the world!"

As we sped over the bridge there was a thick early morning mist on the river and the horses' manes blew in the wind. In the distance, I could see flames shooting into the sky. We pulled up to a scene of utter chaos. The firemen only had feeble little pumps that were useless against this inferno; the heat was so intense it was melting the brickwork. I tried to ask Bram how it started but he could not hear me above the sound of roaring flames and crashing timber. "Need you ask, it's vandals! Yobs torched three cars in my street last week," said Lee.

"You're forgetting, sweetheart, they don't know the meaning of the words vandal, yob or thug! There ain't any in this day and age."

"Yeah, you're right, must be better than our shithole time."

"This will break Henry's heart," said Bram, who had joined us after talking to the firemen, who were running about like blue-arsed flies. "It had taken forty years to accumulate this great stock of scenery that covers forty-four productions, two hundred and sixty scenes in all. It would take all the scene painters in England five years to replace it all."

"It weren't an insurance job was it, Bram?" asked Lee.

"For Christ's sake, Lee," I said, "Look at the man's face." His face, reflected in the fire, was tired and sad.

"The tragic answer to your question, my dear, is; I had it

insured for £12,000, a fortune in this day, when it was time to review the policies this year Henry made me reduce it to £6,000 because these premises are so secure. At least we thought they were. The arches are isolated, no one lives here. I feel the hand of treachery in this. Henry's enemies have done their evil work and, my god, they have done it well."

"Who d'you suspect?" asked Lee.

"GBS and Archer are full of jealousy and spite towards Henry and it would please them greatly to have a hand in his downfall."

Just then eagle-eyed Lee saw two men trying to sneak out of the yard carrying some large picture frames.

"Hold it right there, scumbags," called Lee.

When we got close, they looked a real pair of villains, poorly dressed and dirty with large caps on their heads. They were both big and in their early twenties, so I gripped my gun but kept it out of sight.

"How did you come by those paintings?" asked Bram.

"We found'em, guv. Honest we did."

"That's not true, and you know it, and as they are intact you must have got them before the fire stated." Turning to us Bram said, "We use them to hang on the walls of scenes in various plays."

"And what's in that jar?" shouted Lee. The second man was

holding some sort of big earthenware jug. Lee moved close then said, "It's petrol! I can smell it!"

"Can't be, Lee. They don't have it." I told her.

"Then it's paraffin! You fucking shitbags, you started this fire. Who you working for?" Her voice was now an aggressive scream. The two men got Lee's message. The nearest one put down the pictures and slowly took out a long knife. I pulled my gun and pointed it at his face. He'd never seen one like it but he knew it was a firearm. Lee, of course, already had her gas gun in hand, not knowing what it was they showed no fear of it.

"Drop your knife, sir, or my friends will kill you. They do not live by our rules, I assure you," said Bram, quietly.

The one still holding the knife started to speak. "Well, sir, I reckon you knows a Mr Archer, he's a paying us 50 guineas. Now, if you'd like to make us a better offer."

"What – to put the fire out? You stupid bastards."

"We can't do that, missus, but we can tell you all about Mr Archer and his friend, then you could gets them to pay for the damage."

"I am not prepared to trade with criminals," said Bram.

"So piss off, now, and leave the pictures," said Lee.

The one holding the jar looked real mad and lunged at Lee's throat saying, "We've 'ad enough of this 'old hag.'"

I could have told him that 'old hag' was about the worst

thing you could call Lee because it questioned her sexiness, and Lee is female vanity at it's worst! She fired the gas spray; he staggered back dropping the jar. I don't know if the gas was ignited by the fire, or if what he had in the jar spilt onto the flames, but in a second he was a human fireball. I watched horrified and sick as he stood, arms outstretched, screaming and burning like some horrendous 'Guy Fawkes'. The firemen flung buckets of water over him, but it made no difference. He turned black and stumbled back into the flames and was gone. His friend dropped the knife and shrieking in fear, turned and ran. Lee, quick as a flash, grabbed my gun and got off two fast shots. She was unprepared for the kick the Browning has; it weighs 32oz and has a 5 inch barrel, so her aim was too high.

The man who was now well out of range stopped and screamed back in fury at Lee. "You murdering she-devil from hell. I swear my revenge for your wickedness this day." Then he stumbled on crying and cursing.

"I'll be waiting for you, shithead! Let me know if you'd like burial or cremation like your mate just had!" Lee yelled after him, then handing me the gun back laughing said, "You know when his mate was burning, I should have said, 'What'a you getting so fired up about!'"

Bram, who looked stunned and deeply shocked said, "I fear

we have not seen the last of that gentleman, Miss Lee."

"Lee," I said, "I've had about enough of you! You're one vicious violent cow!"

"Ahhh! Now that's brilliant," she said, in her 'taking the piss' voice. "I've just noticed those big wings on your back! Listen to Mother Teresa in drag! You'll never dump me because you can't resist me; all I have to do is give you the eye! As for me being violent, tell me something; remember a few nights back I dropped you and your lunatic heroin addict pal Ben off late at the Elephant tube, so you could get to Oxford Circus and walk home from there. Well, the next day in the Standard the headline read: 'Two men found murdered on Bakerloo Line'. They'd been gunned down, shot to pieces! The trains are empty that time of night; people are too scared to travel. Now, tell me, were you mixed up in that?"

I reasoned that if I could bring myself to dump her at some future date, I didn't want a 'woman scorned' who had something big on me because hell would have no fury like Lee's, so I thought 'stall for time', making it harder to prove and it's a cert she knows anyway.

"You're right," I said. She smiled knowing once again her woman's intuition had proved correct. "Except, Ben is off the Big H, he's on methadone. Anyway, we got in the last carriage thinking it was empty, but two junkie muggers were laying low on a seat so we couldn't see them. They were both hooded-up. As soon as the doors slid shut they came running down the gangway at us holding hypo needles full of blood, bawling and screeching that it was AIDS infected. They held the needles about an inch from my throat; I was shit scared. I gave one my watch then my wallet so he was distracted taking out my cash. I knew we were gonna get stabbed with the needles anyway, so I said Ben the 'Walther' – that's the make of gun he carries – he got the message, rolled on the floor firing at the same time. In blind rage, he put eight shots into both the shits. Some bullets smashed the windows, hitting the tunnel wall. We jumped out at the next stop, Lambeth North, there was no one around so we pulled our caps right down to avoid the cameras and I walked home to Beak Street. Ben grabbed a mini cab to his place. That's the awful truth of it, Lee, and I've got the nightmares to prove it." I said.

"So, London has two less slime balls, tough shit for them. If they'd stabbed you with AIDS you'd be dead and some snide lawyer would let them 'walk' or they'd get six months probation at most! Give Ben a medal is wot I says!! And you'll get your reward in bed tonight." she said with a laugh, then added with a wink. "Just call me Monica!"

Bram was looking at us as though we were talking Chinese. An angry crowd was starting to gather, so I told Bram to bring on his blue light – we needed it! He did and we were back in the coach moving, but there was no sound from the horses and out the window everything was shrouded in the same ghostly light. Bram gave a nervous cough and said almost apologetically, "Please forgive me, but I feel the desperate need of a rest from your company. Your ways are beyond my understanding."

"Try dumping us in nowhere time and you'll see how nasty we can be," said Lee icily.

"I invited you both to see my time and enjoy its artistry and elegance, but sadly you brought with you the violence of your own times. I feel that if you were to stay here you would be totally different people and if I may say so, much happier people. But you are my guests and as such will be protected by me. You will, of course, be returned to your present day, all we have to do is go back to the Lyceum where we met and when you go through the door you will find yourself in the street where our journey started. Nothing will have changed."

"At times, Bram, you sound like a mouthpiece," laughed Lee.

"She means a lawyer," I explained, before Bram could ask.

"You're quite correct, Miss Lee. I trained as one in Dublin and was called to the bar, but never took it up. I came to London instead and fell in love with the Lyceum and the world of theatre."

"You know, Bram," I said, "Henry is a great talent, maybe the greatest, and the same goes for Ellen and all the others we've met, but I don't think they could have made it without you in the background. You made it all tick and for around 30 years at that."

"Thank you, sir, you're most kind," he said modestly, then added laughing. "Yet, I feel that Mr Shakespeare would have still succeeded without my help!"

"It would have been nice to see Henry and Ellen again," said Lee.

"Well, Henry gave you an open invitation," replied Bram. "I can arrange for you to spend a last day with them in, let me see, 1901. They are doing the last Shakespearean revival at the Lyceum, but are taking a weekend off at Ellen's cottage in Winchelsea."

"Where's that?" I asked.

"On the Sussex coast, a quite delightful little place. When you step out of the coach you will be there. I really don't think you will find any use for your violence and firearms there. Just tell me by thought when you want to return and I will bring you back instantly."

"OK, Bram. One more trip then I want modern day, but don't think it hasn't been fun. Things won't ever be the same back in the present, wherever that is!"

As soon as I'd said that Lee and I stepped from the coach into the sunshine of a quaint ancient town, but no winding streets, in fact, laid out on a grid pattern with a church and churchyard at the centre and in the distance the sea. There was an air of real peace about the place. For the first time I saw Lee strolling along, instead of her usual rush. "Where are we headed?" I asked.

"The Strand Gate. It's like an arch over the road out of town and next to it on the left is Tower Cottage, that's Ellen's place."

"I won't be dumb enough to ask how you know the way because we both hear Bram's voice in our minds, right?"

Before I could say more we were at the cottage. A horse and four-wheeled open carriage stood outside in the sun, the horse was busy munching the grass and there was Henry, tall and elegant as ever, at the door smiling, with Ellen behind him.

"Good Lord, my dear fellow, and you my dear, how delightful to see you both again." He said, in that distinctive voice making every word crystal clear.

Tea was laid on for us and we were made so welcome. They both looked older, of course, but the years had been kind to them and that's crucial for actors. While Lee and Ellen sat in the small garden secluded by the ivy-covered wall of the Strand Gate, Henry and I talked.

"How do you stand the punishing hard work? Bram told me you've had pleurisy that put you off the stage for months; there are more American tours planned; you never miss a rehearsal. When not in London you're on stage in one of Britain's other big cities. Why not ease off a little, none of us are getting younger – know what I mean?"

"Well. Well," he said thoughtfully. You never got a flippant rely from him, always a serious answer. Then he continued, "my friends say I am made of whipcord and steel, but the truth of the matter is acting is my passion, my life; I am always thinking of new productions, new ways of approaching a part. A few days here with Ellen, once in a while, are all the rest I need. I would sooner be here talking shop with a friend like you than be away from it all on holiday and I have such marvellous friends, you know. Theatre is in my blood, my very soul, I never want to retire; I want to die in harness when my time comes, like that, I would go!" With that he snapped his fingers, laughed and said, "And I hope I am on stage at the time."

I was enjoying the company of these two friendly people; there was a modesty about them. That's strange when you know they are superstars of their time and world famous through sheer talent! There's no silly pretentious airs and graces that we get from the five-minute wonders of our time.

"Come, I'll show you over my house," called Ellen.

The place was as pretty as a picture postcard. Flower filled, secluded garden with a cat curled up next to a tortoise on the lawn; and inside, cosy rooms with lots of pictures of her son and daughter, her parents and famous stage people, but not one of her. She had a bird in a cage that hung in the open window, singing away with a heart as free as if he were in the open air, and a yapping terrier like the one that Henry once had. Lee leant against the open latticed window of an upstairs bedroom and sighed. "Wow! Take a look at this view!"

I did, and saw fields full of lambs stretching for miles and in the distance, under a blue cloudless sky, the sea dotted with tiny fishing boats. Away to the left on a hill the small town of Rye, with it's slowly turning windmills.

"I find it so peaceful here," said Ellen.

"It's much more than that, Ellen, its peace of mind," Lee replied quietly, as though thinking aloud.

"What a lovely day it is, come we shall go for a ride. Henry get Tommy from the stable."

Lee and I assumed rightly that Tommy was her horse. We climbed into the back seats and while Henry fixed the horse into the shafts Lee leant close and said in a whisper. "Did you notice their bedrooms have a connecting door?"

"So?" I replied.

"So! You dozy sod, they're lovers – they use this place as an away from it all 'love nest'. I'd like to stay the night, then I could put a glass to the wall and hear them making love!"

"For Christ's sake, Lee!" I replied, "Who gives a shit. Next you'll be telling me you saw a mirror on Ellen's bedroom ceiling and they met via a contact mag! Or maybe they're just friends who screw now and then. When two people act together like they do, there has to be love or it wouldn't come across the footlights the way it does. I'm pleased for them, they're two lovely people with an overload of style and charm."

"OK! OK! So I'm a crude, sexy, know nothing bitch and you're Prince Charming." She then fell about laughing.

With Henry at the reins, we moved off into the sunshine. "Hold it!" shouted Lee. "You've left your cottage door wide open."

Ellen turned and looked at us in surprise saying, "Why ever not, my dears, on such a warm day?"

"Yeah, of course," replied Lee, realising that burglary was unheard of in this age.

Looking back over her shoulder Ellen said, "I love that cottage, it is a million miles from London."

You can say that again I thought and what's with this cottage thing, to me it looks like a two storey house with plenty of rooms.

Ellen started doing the guided tour. "Over there is the church of St Thomas, we go there at night to rehearse our Shakespeare. It's huge inside, like a theatre. Ah! There's Mr Stileman; Henry do give him a wave. He is our Mayor; I help him run the local amateur dramatic society. I have another larger house a few miles away, near Tenterden in Kent called 'Smallhythe.'"

Bram's voice came into my head saying, "That place in your time is a museum dedicated to her memory."

"I've been reading about all the great parts you've played." lied Lee, who never read a book in her life – she'd looked up Ellen's career on her laptop. "You're known as the greatest actress in the world. You've played Ophelia, Portia, Desdemona, Juliet and Lady Macbeth."

Ellen laughed saying, "Thank you, Lee, but do tell me why are you called by such a strange name."

Lee looked surprised and said, "My real name is a strange old one. It's Letitia, I was named after my great grandmother, so they call me Lee for short."

Ellen looked puzzled and said, "That is very odd, my dear. I know several ladies called Letitia, but they are all called Letty for short."

The conversation petered out because we all started to feel uneasy with the way Henry was shifting us along at a fair old speed. We were out in the lanes now, but the horse was going flat out!

Ellen cried, "I know you like to go fast, Henry, but have a care."

Then Lee yelled. "For fuck's sake hit the brakes. Mind those kids!!"

Up ahead, about 200 yards, I saw two little girls standing in the middle of the road with a donkey. Henry stood up pulling back on the reins with all his might. I leant over, grabbed the brake slamming it on to lock the wheels. The whole lot swung across the road sideways, tilted as though we were going over, then smashed back on its wheels with a crash in a cloud of dust. When that dust settled our horse and their donkey were standing nose to nose.

Henry went ballistic. "You stupid children, what on earth are you doing? Never! Never, walk in the road like that again."

Then Lee took over like always. "Stop being a prick, Henry, you were out of order speeding. You're doing your nut because if these kids had been hurt it would be in the papers tomorrow and your cosy love nest would be blown and in this day and age both your showbiz careers would be down the tubes, right? Now, both of you go back to the cottage and have a couple or ten brandies, we'll take the kids home."

Too dazed to work out what she was saying or to argue they

moved off slowly. The youngest of the girls was crying her eyes out. The oldest, who looked about six, was holding her sister tight with one hand and the donkey with the other.

Lee asked their names saying, "Come on, no one's been hurt. Let's go and meet your mum."

I lifted them up onto the old brown donkey and we made our way back to Winchelsea. On the way Kath, the oldest, told me that Gypsy, the donkey, was the family pet and everybody loved him. Their mother turned out to be a widow trying to earn a living as an artist. She thanked us for bringing the kids home safe, and gave Lee a painting she had just finished of Ellen Terry's house. I was surprised how well Lee hit it off with the kids, chatting and laughing with them. After some tea, we said goodbye to this nice little family, then took a stroll around the quaint old place, and as we sat on a seat looking over the churchyard the setting sun told me this strange journey was coming to an end.

"Time to return, Bram," I said. With that the blue light and we were back in Bram's small, untidy office at the Lyceum. "How does it end for Henry?" I asked.

"As the years pass, his health fails, he loses control of his beloved Lyceum, and Ellen takes on solo work. The last years are lonely and hard, but he never stops touring the world and is loved beyond all others by the public. An hour after coming off the stage in Bradford, at ten minutes to twelve on Friday, 13th October in 1905, he dies of a heart attack aged 67. Walter and I will be with him."

"Bram," I said, "he told me a couple of hours ago that's just the way he wanted it."

Bram smiled. "He is buried in Poets Corner, Westminster Abbey. The funeral was massive. London came to a standstill, rather like in your time some years ago when Princess Diana was assassinated in Paris."

"Was she?" asked Lee, in shocked surprise.

"Yes, indeed, she was, but I'll tell you more of that when we meet again in another lifetime. Anyway, the show of public grief was the same."

"All I can say, Bram, is looking at his life he probably was the greatest actor and star of all time. Thanks for showing it all to us. Now we have to return to our own time, but you and the people we've met will stay in our hearts."

"I understand," said Bram, then he spoke a quotation. "A savage loves his native shore."

"Hold it right there, Mr Bigmouth, you can count this savage right out!" said Lee, getting up from her chair. "What have I got to return for? I live in a stinking tower block on a run down, no-go estate where murders, suicides and rapes run at over a hundred a week. I take my life in my hands every time I go out.

Yardies and Russian Mafia run the streets and the law's on their side. I dance naked for men in low down clubs to earn enough to pay my council tax. And when my tits start to sag and younger girls come along then what? The UK's the armpit of the world. Ask yourself what the hell do you have to go back for?"

I looked at her, thinking 'this is a windup', she can't be serious, but knowing her as I did, I felt scared. "Don't talk crazy, Lee. Think about a world with no antibiotics, no anaesthetics and no TV!"

"Total crap!" She spat back at me. "Don't give me any of that PC shit! My sister died lying on a trolley in a hospital corridor where she'd been for a week without treatment. What good did modern medicine do her? As for TV; 24/7 of dumbing down, social brainwashing, mind numbing garbage. Who the fuck needs it? And it can only get worse. Here, I can live with style and enjoy life without fear. Ellen says she can get me stage work."

"I don't see much call for Edwardian pole dancers, Lee." I teased, trying to laugh her out of this madness. "Bram, make her see sense, tell the crazy cow the danger she's facing."

He got up from the table where he'd been writing down more calculations. He studied them carefully, then gripping my arm said, "With the best will in the world, my dear friend, I cannot you see she will have a better life in my time than yours. Indeed, it is you that will have to face extreme danger in the next few years…"

"Oh yeah, like what's on the cards for me – I'll buy it?" I said trying to sound confident.

He looked at me sadly, and then started to speak slowly. "I see a 'Trojan Horse', the enemy is within the gates. The people will be betrayed by traitorous leaders. I see civil war on the streets of London. I see those streets full of dead, struck down by a black death that has been deliberately let loose on the people and made legal by a hated judiciary."

"OK, when that happens I'll jump in the Chrysler and head for the country," I said, still trying to sound casual, but sounding stupid instead.

"That will not be possible. You have a wide road that surrounds London, do you not?" he asked.

"Yeah, you're right, Bram. We call it the M25," said Lee, who in her weird way was fascinated by all this.

"That road will become a ring of steel, lined by soldiers with orders to shoot down anyone who tries to leave or enter the city. The people will be given the means to end their agony."

"Christ! D'you mean suicide tablets?" asked Lee.

"Yes, and euthanasia will be made compulsory for the elderly and you will live to see the word 'elderly' mean 50 years of age! And those who are ill or infirm will suffer the same fate. This will come about because of massive food and housing shortages. The all-seeing eye that watches your movements – what do you call it?"

Once again Lee jumped in. "You mean the CCTV cameras?"

"Yes, they already watch you at work and on the streets. They will be introduced into your homes and made able to hear your speech, so every second of your life you will be watched and listened to. And all will be stamped with the mark of the 'Beast' – an identifying number. There is much worse to tell you, but I do not have time. If you want to leave, then you must do so now, my calculations show that our parallel lifetimes will not be this way again for centuries. For your own sake, my friend, I implore you to stay."

"Lee! For God's sake, come with me." I begged.

She put her arms around me for a last lingering kiss and whispered. "Be lucky."

"Wait", said Bram. "I told you in the coach that I would never reveal just how you die. Now I must. Not many years after your return you will exist in a vicious new world order. You will be arrested by Euro police for trying to cross from one London zone to another without their permission. You will be handed over to the 'Bureau of Social Thinking' and tried in a foreign tongue making it impossible for you to defend yourself. Along with many others you will be sentenced to death and beheaded in Trafalgar Square. Public executions will take place there every Sunday."

I started to say you can't be serious but stopped when I saw the tears in his eyes. "Can I avoid that fate Bram?", I asked.

"Yes. As I explained you can change both the past and the future and that is why I have forewarned and so forearmed you, but it will not be without risk. Trust no-one and tell no-one your views. Spies will be everywhere. If you must return to your evil time you will be beyond my help. Lee and I will pray for you."

I turned and ran towards the Lyceum exit, now shrouded in that misty blue light.

My head spun violently and I started to fall down, down, down to the bottom of the world. I reached out and steadied myself against a concrete pillar. It was dark and raining. I pressed my watch and my ever-faithful oriental girlfriend told me it was just gone 5am. No matter what happened to me she always sounded cool and calm. So it was only about four hours ago when Bram first spoke to us. The pillar I was holding up was one of those outside the Lyceum. I was back!

The Chrysler was still parked over the road, but what the hell's happened to it? When I got close, I could see it was burnt black; those great white wall tyres were now hanging off the rims, a mass of smouldering rubber. Some of the windows had cracked with the heat. I wanted to cry but stopped myself because a police car pulled in and two robo cops walked over.

"We've been wondering when you'd show. Your car is it?"

"Yeah, looks like bastard yobs have torched it."

"More unusual than that," said robo one. "In last night's freak storm it got struck by lightning." He looked bored and bad tempered with the rain running off the brim of his cap. "So get it moved before 8 am or we take it to the car pound and it costs a fortune to get it back. This is a no parking zone!" With that they got back in their car and sped off.

I called after them. "You dumbed down pricks, in a hurry to catch up on the soaps are we? Can't you see this is a rare classic?" Now I knew for sure I was back in the present. I yanked the door open and reached inside the glove compartment for Lee's bag where she kept her mobile and there was the envelope that Pad had given us when we dropped him off. I looked around inside the car, and to my amazement the interior had not been touched by the fire, so I got in out of the rain. Lee's bag felt heavy; looking inside I saw the reason – a small gun! What the hell was she doing with that? On closer inspection I recognised it as a 2" snub nose Smith & Wesson 36. It holds five shots and this one's fully loaded, only weighs about 20 ounces. Adequately powerful enough to put a mugger down if standing close, and for Lee, very easy to hide in a handbag.

I scrolled through the numbers on her mobile until I got to Delroy – maybe he'd help.

"Hell, man, don't cha know the time. What'a you on?"

I then told him about the great time Lee and me had at his last party and my situation right now with the car and if he came and got me he'd get the repair job and make a lotta cash from the insurance. The last part got him.

"Hang right on, man, I'll be there."

As I sat waiting, I thought about Lee and how we'd sat in this car while the thunder crashed outside and she looked up Henry Irving on the Internet with her laptop. I tried not to think of never seeing her again because I don't think I can face it. Then I remembered dear old Pad's photo. I opened the envelope. I'd had more than my share of mystery this past few hours, but this one really hit me. Like Pad said, it was an old photo of Henry and Bram entering the Lyceum with two other people. Yeah! And those two were me and Lee! Henry, Bram and I did not appear to notice the camera, but Lee was smiling into the lens looking gorgeous in a long silk dress and a huge hat covered in flowers. I was wearing a long stylish coat. We both looked the business. Why did I return, what good will it be here without her? I dozed for a while then woke to find the street lit up by a brilliant flashing orange light. Delroy had arrived with his massive car transporter.

"I smell burning, man, and I also smell money," he laughed, showing those gold fillings that glinted in the orange light. "Be happy, man, she'll be as good as new in a couple of weeks, you have my word."

The crane swung my classic old car up onto the trailer, where Del secured it with chains then said, "Don't walk home in the rain, man, you look dead on your feet. There ain't no black cabs to be had at this time, so ride back with me. My lady will make you breakfast and I'll fix you up with some new wheels."

As we crossed Waterloo Bridge, I could hear the faint chimes of Big Ben telling me it was 7am, even above the ear splitting beat of the rap music he had going full blast all the way to Brixton! I felt better after some toast and at least a thousand cups of tea! Then went out into the yard to see my car up on a ramp, with Del already working on it. Looking around his repair yard was always interesting because he dealt with rare motors. Over by the gates stood a stately Rolls with a bashed in door, next to it a really Bogart-looking Buick Skylark. In the spray shop was a gleaming 3.8 S-Type Jag with no engine. Then my eye fell on a bright red MG Sports. How Lee would have loved that one. A wave of heartbreak swept over me as I realised I was already thinking of her in the past tense.

Del came over wiping his hands on some rag. Then putting his hand on my shoulder said, "I can tell you're hurting, man, well this is gonna place a smile back on your face, take a look at this baby."

With that he lifted the up-and-over door of one of the lockups. There stood a long, two-tone, powerful looking four-door saloon with huge silver headlamps and distinctive rivets or studs all along the squared bodywork.

"It's sure in showroom condition, what the hell is it, an Alvis?" I asked.

"No, man, even you won't know this one. It's a Railton. She's one of the last big ones they made in 1938."

"Real elegant, Del, but she's British, you know I only drive Yankie!"

"Don't be racist, man!" He laughed, showing those gold fillings again. "Just cos it ain't flying the stars and stripes. Now you hear this, under that hand built English body there's a four litre straight eight Hudson power unit, so you're talking solid Detroit muscle! That's grabbed yer by the balls right? Still, makes a change from Lee doing it, I guess. Talking of that singing bird, where is she?" He asked, handing me the Railton's keys.

"Not sure, Del, I'm dead worried about her."

"She'll be OK, I sold her a small ladies gun months ago and showed her how to use it. With respect, man, she'd be one very dangerous lady to cross."

I turned the ignition key and the eight cylinders fired first time with a roar. Del listened carefully for a minute then said, "She's ticking like a clock. Enjoy man 'til I get old American Joe back on the road, then we'll talk money."

Before closing the door, I slapped his raised hand, told him he was a real pal and thanked him. I drove it carefully back to the West End and tucked it away over in Cork Street in Mayfair, thinking it would be safer there from vandals on a Saturday night than in Soho. As I let myself in the street door I looked up and high on the wall the words 'Erected 1882' were still there. On my landing lay Snowball, the white cat belonging to the people downstairs, who were away. I remembered how Lee had screamed abuse at them for leaving him last time. I picked him up and carried him in with me, put down some food and milk, poured myself a couple of whiskies then took a real hot shower, lay on my bed where Lee and I had made love so many times and slept an uneasy dream filled sleep. When I woke it was dark, I stood by the window for some time just looking out over the rainsoaked rooftops, then the phone rang. It was Bob Appleby.

"I've got some sad news for you and Lee." I knew what he

was going to say. "Paddy Regan died early this morning," he said quietly.

"He was a great guy, I shall miss him," I replied. What else could I say? Yes I know Bram Stoker told me in 1878! For the want of something better to do I thought I'd check my e-mails. I deleted the usual porn junk mail, read a few business ones, then my heart raced when I saw that the next one was from Lee! My fingers trembled on the mouse as I opened it up. It read…'My last e-mail. Batteries almost out and no way can I recharge. Remember the scenery fire? Well friend of Guy Fawkes is giving me severe aggro and blackmailing me dry. If I can't meet next payment he says he'll kill me. Bram says according to his Egyptian gods our lifetimes will cross one last time after midnight tonight, but only for under an hour. I have a gun in my handbag. It's in the Chrysler. Bring it with you. Bram says he can get me to Waterloo Bridge just past midnight, when I'll explain all. Still love you. 'SOTLBALL' XXX.' In a daze I printed it out and turned the computer off, then sat reading and re-reading it. Did it mean I'd have a second chance to join her back in the past? This time I'd take it. The oriental girl said it was 11.25 pm. I grabbed Lee's handbag and was down the stairs like a flash and running towards Regent Street. When I opened the Railton's door the strong smell of leather from the old seats hit me. As I passed Henry's statue on my way to the Strand I called out 'wish me luck 'H' cos you started all this'. I drove slowly over the bridge, but saw nothing, circled round and parked on the bridge near the National Film Theatre facing the embankment and waited. By now it was gone 1.00 am, the traffic was very quiet even for the early hours of a Sunday morning. Oh no, don't say I've missed her. I got out and walked towards the middle of the bridge. It was getting cold and misty and I could no longer see the lights on the embankment. Then I heard it, faint at first, but yes, it sounded like the clip-clop of a horse. I looked back to where I'd parked the Railton, then I saw it in the distance approaching slowly, the horse and carriage were jet black; the horse had a prancing step with it's head held high. The driver was wrapped in a black cloak; fear of the unknown hit me in the guts. Instinctively, I reached for my Browning and panicked when I knew I'd left it back at the flat. Still, at least I had Lee's 38.

The carriage had now stopped, but the horse was restless causing the carriage to move back and forth. I reached for the door handle to get in, but to my horror my hand went right through! It was like trying to grab hold of smoke! The driver spoke and to my relief it was Bram!

"No, you cannot join us, my old friend, you made your decision and it is final. I wish, sir, it could be otherwise. If those charts drawn by the pharaohs thousands of years ago are correct, then I estimate we have less than half an hour of each other's company."

Lee was at the window looking lovely, but older! Gone was the hi-gloss lipstick and heavy eye shadow. She had on the large hat with flowers that I'd seen in Pad's photo.

"Let me do the talking, darling," she said in that soft sexy voice. "Things are going real great for me. I've taken over from Nellie Farran at the Gaiety Theatre just round the corner from the Lyceum. I'm a very big star and the money's rolling in. I've bought a big house in Stanhope Street off Bayswater Road."

"Lee! Lee! You're doing my head in, what are you on about. I left you less than 24 hours ago!" I shouted at her.

"In your time, yes, but in mine two years have passed. My singing and dancing made me famous, then that bastard comes out of the woodwork and puts the bite on me for money. If the story of his pal burning to death because of me gets out it'll be the end of me. He comes to the stage door every night for money, hangs around outside my house, that's why I need my gun, the gas spray ran out ages ago. You're the only one I'd trust for a thing like this. That's why I've come back; don't let him take it all away from me. Help me one last time, please, darling."

Just looking at her made me feel disorientated. "I'll do

anything, you know that I miss you so much, Lee," I said, handing her the handbag.

"Thanks, darling. See, I still wear my cobra." She held out her wrist with the bracelet curled around it. "And here's a present for you, no use to me, I can't plug it into a gas lamp." She handed me the laptop.

Just then the horse moved back with a start, causing me to jump clear of the wheels. What had startled the animal was a big rough looking man heading towards us.

"It's him, Miss Lee," shouted Bram. "He is not aware of it, but he has crossed time with us."

"There was no money waiting for me this week, my fine lady." he yelled. "You're in for a severe beating, you won't be dancing for many a day!" Then looking at me shouted. "Ah! We meet again gov'nor, but this time I have the pistol." With that he drew some sort of old one shot duelling pistol from his belt, aimed at me and fired. After the flash, the force of the hit knocked me to the ground but the laptop took the full blast! Having only one shot he put the gun back in his belt and took out a short nasty looking club, standing over me he raised it about to smash my head in. Lee leant right out the coach window, holding her small gun in both hands US cop style and taking careful aim, from a range of only about ten feet started firing at his head and that's where the first bullet struck, just above the ear. With an agonising scream he dropped the club and put his hand to his head, turned to her and gasped one last word 'mercy'.

"Not here, scumbag!" she yelled. "You made the mistake of coming into the 21st century, you're outta yer class and now you'll pay for it. Yeah, you've had yer last meal ticket." With that she began firing again, slowly and viciously, every shot hitting his face. Blood and chips of bone flew into the air. The horse rose up on his hind legs at the sound of gunfire. Bram turned away in disgust and shock. Finally the gun was empty, the victim had staggered backwards, across the pavement and was now sprawled out on the low railings of the bridge, for all the world like a beaten boxer hanging on the ropes!

"That just proves," said Lee laughing, "no one fucks with me unless I want them to! We've gotta move, Tel, or be trapped here. Get rid of him and the evidence. Hey, I can imagine tomorrow's headlines: 'Victorian yob found in Thames carrying expensive laptop and heavy club.'" With that she blew me a kiss as the coach pulled away.

I felt sick as I tried to lift the poor devil over the railings; his face was a mass of mangled flesh, no eyes or nose left and blood everywhere. He weighed about 14 stone, so I had to strain with all my might to tip him over. He hit the water with a huge splash, floated face down for a second or so then nothing, gone forever. I picked up his club and slung it after him. The laptop's strong case had a hole in the side you could put your fist through, so that went over too.

The coach was disappearing fast, but through the oval back window I could still see the colourful flowers on Lee's hat. Then, in a moment of madness I knew I had to try one last time to keep her. I dashed back to the Railton and in less than 30 seconds the Detroit muscle had me tailgating her coach. I don't know what I had planned in my confused mind, maybe force them over and drag Lee out or go with her! The horse had broken into a fast gallop, but at the last minute veered to the left away from the underpass, probably scared of entering the dark tunnel. I accelerated into the underpass like a tornado and a couple of minutes later came out on to the wide Kingsway and screeched to a stop blocking the Strand Lane, then waited as they came the long way round by the Aldwich. The car has one of those old spot lights fixed to the side of the roof so you can direct the beam from inside the car, I turned it to face their direction, then in the distance saw them coming at a hell of a pace and heading right for me. I switched on the powerful spot light and lit the horse and carriage in a blaze of golden aura, but the weirdest thing of all was they were now coming at me from across the sands of a desert under, a brilliant sun with pyramids in the background and a crowd of outriders dressed like ancient Egyptians carrying banners and spears. They rode in a close protective formation around Lee's coach. On the banners that blew in the hot desert wind was a strange symbol in gold and black of a long snake like Lee's bracelet and an evil looking bird with huge wings. It was a scene to strike the fear of god into anyone. Too late to reverse out of the way, the horses eyes looked wild and crazy as they smashed into the car, but there was no impact! No sound! We became computer images superimposed on each other's time. For a split second Lee was in the car with me, then I in the coach with her! She brushed my face with her hand and as our lips met said, "We'll meet again in another lifetime, so don't pine for me. Bye for now my darling and thanks."

"No, thank you, Lee." I replied trying to hold on to her with all my might, but the force of time pulling her from me was too great and she was gone.

Chapter Four

Back at the flat Snowball was curled up on my bed. I didn't fancy whisky, so made some tea and tried to think about all that had happened, but it was beyond me and I felt depressed and exhausted. I turned on the computer, this time there were no e-mails, but I searched the net for over an hour looking at Egyptology sites. Then I found what I was looking for; the symbol that I'd seen on those flags and banners, a huge curling snake, it's head entwined or maybe being attacked by a ferocious bird of prey. The web page told me it's the sign of the Egyptian God 'WADJET', the Royal Cobra Goddess. A war and desert goddess who can control time and will guard and protect with extreme violence if need be. Those born under her sign (28th October to 26th November), on their never-ending journey across the universe they will live many lives, sometimes crossing from one lifetime to another. Women of this sign are often beautiful and always passionate lovers, but have a dangerous and unpredictable nature.

I shut down and decided my tea did need a dash of whisky because I knew for sure Lee's birthday was in mid-November! As I sat thinking about it all, one thing did occur to me; all the places that Bram had shown us – the Lyceum, Henry's flat near Bond Street, even the fire in Southwark, I knew all those areas.

All except one – Winchelsea! Until these incredible events I'd never been there or even heard of the place. So, if I returned there now and recognised it then I must have been there before and that could only be with Lee when Ellen Terry lived there.

My road map showed me I wanted the Hastings road – 1066 and all that! Then swing east along the coast for about eight miles. I put my blood covered clothes in a bin liner; took another shower; had some more tea and put more milk down for Snowball then I was off, stopping only to put the clothes in a litter bin. I couldn't face Waterloo Bridge again so cut out over Westminster. The early Sunday morning South London traffic was light and I was soon on the M25 that one day Bram said would become a ring of steel lined with troops. I decided to blow the cobwebs out of my head and pressed down the accelerator. Del wasn't kidding; the Railton's performance was awesome! It was outside lane all the way and screw the speed cameras! I had to flash a couple of poncey Mercs and BMs to move over and a biker in black leathers driving a great looking machine took me on for about five miles, but as my speedo needle moved towards 135 mph he flashed his lights and dropped back in defeat. The suspension was much harder than my Chrysler and the steering wasn't exactly precise. I know Del had done a lot of updating on it, but considering it was around 70 years old – well as Lee would say – for fuck's sake this is one wicked set of wheels!!

Less than two hours after leaving Soho, I pulled into the ancient little town of Winchelsea second time around! I parked by the Museum near the Strand Gate and it all looked virtually the same, the church and churchyard, the layout of the small roads. The only difference was a few cars but no horses and one or two tourists with cameras. I recognised it all as I guess in my heart I expected to. Ellen's Tower Cottage had changed in a few ways. The fence around it was higher and the small gate was now over on the left and what looked like an extension had been added, but it had kept its charm. Ellen would still love it. In my mind's eye I could see Henry, Ellen, Lee and me coming out of the door laughing as we got into the carriage to go for a ride that sunny day so long ago.

I knew I couldn't go on like this, maybe I'd sell the Chrysler to Del, wrap up the business and the flat and get some Spanish sun for a year or two. I stopped daydreaming with a jolt when I heard Bram's voice.

"You have been drawn to Winchelsea, my friend, for a reason. Call and see a very elderly lady by the name Katharina Forbes-Dunlop. No time to talk more, our lifetimes are moving away from each other at the rate of millions of years a second and I am desperately short of time because this year, 1912, is the year of my death. No need for concern, old friend, we all die and are born many times and we shall surely meet again. I may have time for one more short message and then the rest will be silence!"

"Bram!" I said quickly. "I promise you I'll read Dracula." I heard his laughter fading away into oblivion.

I tapped 192 into my mobile, got her number and wrote it on the back of my hand. When a woman's voice answered I said I was writing a book about all the famous people who'd lived here over the years and an interview with Mrs Forbes-Dunlop would be a great help.

She asked me to hold on. Then came back to say, "Yes, Kath will see you, but don't stay too long; she is a great age and tires easily." Then directed me to a house called the 'Glebe' only five minutes walk away.

I was shown into a big room and there was Kath sitting on a large window seat. We shook hands and made some small talk.

"I'm nearly a 100, you know," she said smiling.

Well, no way did she look it. I told her truthfully she could pass for 70. Some tea was brought in on a silver tray and as we began to talk. I got the impression she had never worked on the checkout at Tescos or lived in a Peckham tower block.

She then confirmed this by saying, "I've lived in Winchelsea all my life." And mentioned all the famous people who had lived there. The writer Joseph Conrad, the artist Mallias and many more, finally she got around to Ellen Terry and Henry Irving. "They almost ran my sister and I down one day," she laughed. "Here, have a look at this photo." Handing me an old worn sepia coloured photo of two young girls standing next to a donkey. Now I knew why Bram had told me to make this visit.

"So, that's you with your little sister and your pet donkey, Gypsy. It's a lovely picture," I said.

She put the photo back in the album with great care, and then looking at me for a long time smiled and spoke a quotation. "'There is a bond between us which dates before today. We are not strangers.' You gave yourself away by knowing the name of my beloved old donkey, Gypsy. I never told you and no one living could have told you. Like all old people, I recall my childhood in perfect detail, but if you ask me about last week, I've forgotten!"

To try and answer her I said, "If I told you the man who took you home that day was my great grandfather, who I look very much like, would you believe me?"

She smiled again and said. "No, I would not, so don't try to explain the unexplainable! I recall that day you and Letty walked us home very well. We saw a lot of her in later years.

She would often visit Ellen at Tower Cottage. Henry was, of course, dead by then. I recall one day we asked about you, she looked so wistful and I have always remembered her strange reply, 'Oh he decided to live a very different sort of life in another world. If you live to be a very old lady you might see him again one day and if you do, tell him I made the right decision. I hope he did and please give him my love.'"

We both finished our tea in silence with tears in our eyes. When she spoke again it was another quotation. "There are more things in heaven and earth, Horatio, than are dreamt of in your philosophy."

I paused then came back with one of my own. "O'call back yesterday. Bid time return."

"She became a great star, you know. Letty ended up far richer than Ellen."

"Letty? You mean Lee?"

"No, I mean Letty, Letty Lind. You see that big book over on the shelf between the two smaller ones, get it down; it has her photo in it.

The book was a very large slim hardback, full of colour plate photos of actors and actresses with a write up under each picture. The title, in gold letters, was 'Celebrities of the Stage' Published by Newnes Ltd 1901. There was Henry, dressed in the red robes of Cardinal Wolsey and all the rest of the stars of the time. Half way into the book I nearly dropped it with shock. There was a full page photo of Lee looking gorgeous in a heavy silk dress with tight waist and full sleeves holding a small bunch of flowers in her white gloved hands, another huge hat covered in white feathers, a swept up hair style and a 'butter wouldn't melt in her mouth' expression. Stunned I sat down and started to read the write up: 'Letty Lind, successor to Nellie Farran, a wonderful actress and charming dancer now a great star at the Gaiety Theatre. Tremendous hit in *Cinder-Ellen* and a sensation in *The Geisha*. Letty has no equal on the London stage today. Real name Letitia Rudge born in Birmingham now lives in London. Has recently purchased a magnificent town house off the Bayswater Road where she gives parties attended by the most famous in the land etc etc.'

I replaced the book on the shelf. "Would you like to keep it?" asked Kath.

"Yes I would, I'll treasure it, thank you"

We walked slowly to the door, I kissed her hand and said goodbye.

"That's just what Irving would have done," she said and we both laughed, then she asked. "Before you go, answer Letty's question for me. Did you make the right decision?"

I thought carefully then replied. "No, I made the biggest

mistake of my life, but now it's too late, over a century too late!"

As I stepped into the bright sunshine Bram's voice came to me once more and for the last time saying…"The trumpets summon us, and the drums beat the time of the onward march – quick or slow as duty calls. March! March! March!"

"Time is – Time was – Time is past."

TODAY there is a plaque on the wall of Bram's house in Chelsea saying the author of Dracula once lived here and there's one on the wall of Henry's place in Mayfair saying the great actor lived there. There is a museum dedicated to Ellen at Smallhythe in Kent and her Tower Cottage is still in Winchelsea. The Dogs Cemetery was removed from Hyde Park in 1934 and the words 'Erected in 1882' are still above the pub in Beak Street. The Adelphi Theatre is doing great business and the alley leading up to Maiden Lane where Bill Terriss was murdered still runs alongside it. Even the railway arches where the scenery went up in flames in Southwark are still there. The Lyceum Theatre, after a massive facelift, is once again one of the busiest and one of the most beautiful theatres in London and, yes, Henry's statue still stands watching and maybe waiting at the end of Irving Street.